HONOR THE FALLEN

SEAL Brotherhood: Legacy Series

Book 2

SHARON HAMILTON

SHARON HAMILTON'S BOOK LIST

SEAL BROTHERHOOD BOOKS

SEAL BROTHERHOOD SERIES

Accidental SEAL Book 1

Fallen SEAL Legacy Book 2

SEAL Under Covers Book 3

SEAL The Deal Book 4

Cruisin' For A SEAL Book 5

SEAL My Destiny Book 6

SEAL of My Heart Book 7

Fredo's Dream Book 8

SEAL My Love Book 9

SEAL Encounter Prequel to Book 1

SEAL Endeavor Prequel to Book 2

Ultimate SEAL Collection Vol. 1 Books 1-4 /2 Prequels

Ultimate SEAL Collection Vol. 2 Books 5-7

SEAL BROTHERHOOD LEGACY SERIES

Watery Grave Book 1

Honor The Fallen Book 2

BAD BOYS OF SEAL TEAM 3 SERIES

SEAL's Promise Book 1

SEAL My Home Book 2

SEAL's Code Book 3

Big Bad Boys Bundle Books 1-3

BAND OF BACHELORS SERIES

Lucas Book 1

Alex Book 2

Jake Book 3

Jake 2 Book 4

Big Band of Bachelors Bundle

BONE FROG BROTHERHOOD SERIES

New Year's SEAL Dream Book 1

SEALed At The Altar Book 2

SEALed Forever Book 3

SEAL's Rescue Book 4

SEALed Protection Book 5

Bone Frog Brotherhood Superbundle

BONE FROG BACHELOR SERIES

Bone Frog Bachelor Book 0.5

Unleashed Book 1

SUNSET SEALS SERIES

SEALed at Sunset Book 1

Second Chance SEAL Book 2

Treasure Island SEAL Book 3

Escape to Sunset Book 4

The House at Sunset Beach Book 5

Second Chance Reunion Book 6

LOVE VIXEN

Bone Frog Love

SHADOW SEALS

Shadow of the Heart

SILVER SEALS SERIES

SEAL Love's Legacy

SLEEPER SEALS SERIES

Bachelor SEAL

STAND ALONE BOOKS & SERIES

SEAL's Goal: The Beautiful Game

Nashville SEAL: Jameson

True Blue SEALS Zak

Paradise: In Search of Love

Love Me Tender, Love You Hard

NOVELLAS

SEAL You In My Dreams Magnolias and Moonshine

PARANORMALS

GOLDEN VAMPIRES OF TUSCANY SERIES

Honeymoon Bite Book 1

Mortal Bite Book 2

Christmas Bite Book 3

Midnight Bite Book 4

THE GUARDIANS

Heavenly Lover Book 1

Underworld Lover Book 2

Underworld Queen Book 3

Redemption Book 4

FALL FROM GRACE SERIES

Gideon: Heavenly Fall

NOVELLAS

SEAL Of Time Trident Legacy

All of Sharon's books are available on Audible, narrated by the talented J.D. Hart.

ABOUT THE BOOK

Out of the depths of loss comes a glowing shadow...
A modern miracle of science restores a family but threatens marriages.
A new alliance is forged, with a love more powerful than ever.

Libby and Coop's happy family of four is shattered by news that Libby's mom has terminal cancer. Meanwhile, the past comes back to haunt all of them as Will Brownlee, Libby's uncle and former SEAL who died in Grenada, has fathered a daughter who finds them through DNA testing and presents herself for the first time.

An extreme athlete and the opposite of Libby on so many fronts, she comes between Libby and her husband, as well as her father. In the middle of a family crisis, Cooper is sent back on an emergency deployment, leaving the family unit behind in shambles.

Read this emotional story about love and loss, saying hello and good-bye at the same time, as they all journey on this rocky ride of unpredictable events where control is an illusion.

Will the love they create between them be a strong enough bond to hold this family unit together, or will it explode and fragment into unbelievable pain and loss forever?

Libby and Coop learn about family, and love, and the commitment they hold to themselves, their children, and their legacy, and the risks they must take to have it all.

You won't want to miss this gut-wrenching story of Libby and Cooper and what they will have to do to survive, ten years later when we first met them in Fallen SEAL Legacy.

AUTHOR'S NOTE

I always dedicate my SEAL Brotherhood books to the brave men and women who defend our shores and keep us safe. Without their sacrifice, and that of their families—because a warrior's fight always includes his or her family—I wouldn't have the freedom and opportunity to make a living writing these stories. They sometimes pay the ultimate price so we can debate, argue, go have coffee with friends, raise our children and see them have children of their own.

One of my favorite tributes to warriors resides on many memorials, including one I saw honoring the fallen of WWII on an island in the Pacific:

"When you go home
Tell them of us, and say
For your tomorrow,
We gave our today."

These are my stories created out of my own imagination. Anything that is inaccurately portrayed is either my mistake, or done intentionally to disguise something I might have overheard over a beer or in the corner of one of the hangouts along the Coronado Strand.

I support two main charities. Navy SEAL/UDT Museum operates in Ft. Pierce, Florida. Please learn about this wonderful museum, all run by active and former SEALs and their friends and families, and who rely on public support, not that of the U.S. Government.
www.navysealmuseum.org

I also support Wounded Warriors, who tirelessly bring together the warrior as well as the family members who are just learning to deal with their soldier's condition and have nowhere to turn. It is a long path to becoming well, but I've seen first-hand what this organization does for its warriors and the families who love them. Please give what your heart tells you is right. If you cannot give, volunteer at one of the many service centers all over the United States. Get involved. Do something meaningful for someone who gave so much of themselves, to families who have paid the price for your freedom. You'll find a family there unlike any other on the planet.
www.woundedwarriorproject.org

CHAPTER 1

CALVIN COOPER, BETTER known to his brothers as "Coop," was flying home to San Diego from North Carolina after his two-week SEAL Medic re-certification at Fort Bragg. Sitting beside him was one of his favorite friends, fellow Team 3 medic T.J. Talbot, who was munching on peanuts and staring out at the clouds since he got the window seat.

Both of them were big—Coop tall, nearly 6'4", and T.J., well, he was just big everywhere. Even though technically Coop was senior to him, it wasn't like that between them. T.J. was a few years younger and more agile, and his reaction times were wickedly fast.

T.J. had headsets plugged into his phone, listening to something with a big orchestral background, something dramatic, like Two Steps From Hell, one of their favorites while working out. And with song titles like "Remember The Fallen" or "One Against 1,000" or even "All is Lost," it made for the kind of mood they liked to have on those workouts. Coop had to admit the music did make him feel seven or eight feet tall when his heart swelled as he listened to the moving music.

No one outside the Brotherhood would ever understand that. And anyone who thought there was something wrong with them for listening to such music wasn't ever going to be in Coop's rolodex. He even hoped never to meet such a person.

We are the land of the free, the home of the brave.

If a person didn't believe in that, they didn't deserve to serve in the military, let alone wear a Trident.

He watched the big medic's jaw move under the skin of his clean-shaven face as he considered the clouds and munched on his peanuts silently.

Coop was about to interrupt that silence. He hoped Special Operator Talbot didn't mind too much.

"You ever get nervous coming home?" he asked T.J.

His buddy slowly turned his head, his eyes slightly squint-ed as Coop felt the scan yielding to a full-on expression of disgust. "You started drinking?" he asked.

"Not for ten years now." Coop had developed a drinking problem when he served on an East Coast team and had been involved in an auto accident that nearly took his life. That, along with the breakup with his girlfriend at the time, brought him out west to join SEAL Team 3 with Kyle and the boys.

"Well," T.J. said as he tried to shift in the airplane seat that was way too small for either of them. The pretty gate agent didn't like the way he checked her out and did not give them the Business Class upgrade they asked for. "I was going to make a smart remark about your wife, but we both have women that make us go weak at the knees. So I guess you're talking about that. I just let her see that. I may be wrong, but I think she thinks that's sexy as hell."

"I can see it now. Similar to cold stone fear: mouth parched, tongue sticking to the roof, and huge sweat rings dripping down to your ass-crack. The stuttering, trying to swallow, and struggling with where to put your tongue once it's dislodged. You can't tell me you don't call that nervous?" Coop dished back.

"Oh, it happens that way with me. But then I watch her inhale. I know she can smell the sweat pouring out from everywhere and hear the kettledrums of my heart pressing to burst out of my chest. I look for when her eyelids flutter, and I know it's going to be a memorable evening, afternoon, or morning, depending on when we get in."

Coop nodded and smiled to the headrest of the seat in front of him.

"So you let the nervousness turn you on."

"No, I watch her get turned on, and that turns me on."

"Big distinction. Sorry," Coop said, winking.

"You getting into one of those moods, Coop? You're usually cool as a cucumber. Nothing of your insides shows, man. You chew on ice, drink your mineral water down, and never sweat."

"I'm Scandinavian, T.J. You've watched Sven Tolar? You ever see him nervous around Kelly?"

"I think you're a bit hotter than Sven. He thinks eating pickled herring with sour cream is sexy, and then he chases it down with buttermilk for God's sake. That ain't natural, Coop."

Their friend, a former FSB Norwegian Special Forces

commando, often accompanied them on missions because of his extensive training in Africa while the Americans were pouring out their blood in the Middle East.

And also, because the guys liked him. He was one unflappable SOB.

Coop smiled as he remembered some of the crosstalk at his Nebraska dinner table that summer before he left for the Teams. The boys in high school teased him and his other Scandinavian friends about not getting sufficiently revved up on girls and trucks, as if they were defective.

"You have to whisper nice things to them, Coop, or they'll never come for you."

"How in the world did you get born, Coop? Was your mom implanted with an ear of corn?"

He remembered the church exchange his youth group had with the black A.M.E. church across town, and the experience did nearly bring on a heart attack when he was asked to "testify." That albino preacher with the pink eyes wouldn't give up until he mumbled "Hallelujah," which got him a standing ovation and made him nearly wet his pants. He was sure he had just stood at the gates of Hell and been saved by the blood of Christ.

After that, becoming a Navy SEAL was the easy part. Even getting married and having two kids was easy. Testifying was the hardest thing he'd ever done.

But today, for some strange reason, Coop was nervous to greet his beautiful, brown-eyed wife of eleven years. They'd spent a half day in the course talking about erectile dysfunction and what to do about it if one of the Team Guys came to them for meds. They talked about aging, PTSD, symptoms of mental illness, and signs of denial when someone got injured or wasn't all there mentally. He knew all these things, had trained on them before, but now, at thirty-five years of age, he wasn't looking forward to discovering Libby didn't have the passion for him he needed so badly. It was indeed scary how much he needed her.

And maybe he'd just answered his own question.

T.J. had taken to looking out the window again while Coop thought about how shocked he'd been to learn about the drug use and alcoholism, even among the elite Special Forces. And was he thinking about this because he was toying with the idea that perhaps it would soon be time for him to retire?

That sent a chill down his spine. If he wasn't a SEAL, what would he be? The housewife for the family? Gardener? Taxi Driver? Truck mechanic? Why did that scare him? He had asked Libby to do this just about every day since they had Will and Gillian. Was that fair?

"So you think I should show her I'm scared, then?" he asked T.J., who, once again, turned slowly with attitude.

"Only if you are. Because it would truly be scary for her if you weren't but were trying to act scared."

He had a point there.

Maybe it wasn't fear but a lack of self-confidence. They'd heard so many awful stories this time around. The new instructor was a Marine who took pleasure in trying to shock the Navy SEAL medics in his class. Normally, the course was taught by a SEAL on a special billet or on injured inactive duty, but all the action heroes were out being action heroes, and there weren't any to spare.

"You're right," Coop said before T.J. could return to the view of the clouds.

"What's gotten you twisted up, Coop?"

"Didn't all those stories get to you, even a little bit?"

T.J.'s eyes lit up like the twinkle lights he put on his Christmas tree every year.

"Okay, I got you now. Loud and clear." The big SEAL inhaled and spread his chest, trying to adjust himself in the unforgiving seat. Coop wouldn't have been surprised if the seatbelt burst wide open and the metal latch become a projectile and hit someone in the head.

"Oh, good, because for a while there, I was thinking you were thinking maybe I was crazy. Can't have that," mumbled Coop.

"It's a matter of history. My upbringing is totally different than yours. I was constantly messed with as a kid, by either older foster kids, my crappy foster parents, or the cops I was running away from all the time. It takes a lot for me to feel fear when it comes to coming home, meeting women, or just talking to Team buds. I had an answer or an excuse for everything. I learned how to take care of myself because I was the only person in the universe I could count on. No one else was there. Not like you, with your strong, cultural family unit. I was just another shirt attached with clothespins on the clothesline of life, except I got two old ratty wooden ones, and you got nice, clean plastic ones in bright colors. Nothing about my childhood was pretty."

T.J. wasn't asking for pity. Coop knew he was just telling

him to grow a pair, like he did. Afterall, he married his best friend's widow, who was seven months pregnant at the time, and it took her a whole month before she stopped hating him. That didn't bother T.J. like it would have bothered or even discouraged Coop.

"So you're saying I'm pampered, then?"

"You said that, not me."

"But you believe it."

T.J. frowned in thought. "I'm not sure. But maybe this will make you feel a little better. You're about one of the most level-headed guys I know. And there isn't anyone else I'd prefer going into battle with because I can count on you. You know how to build structure, stability. I know how to improvise."

"You know what I think, T.J.?"

"Hard to say, my friend."

"If you hadn't become a Navy SEAL, you'd have made a damn good philosopher."

"I was kinda thinking I could have been a male escort. I love women. Thank goodness I'm so hopelessly in love with Shannon I don't ever look elsewhere. But damn, I'm good at being patient and then giving her everything I got. I love rocking her world. I like it when she's so overwhelmed with emotion she can't help herself. She's like a racehorse—all beauty and sleekness, fragile, filled with deep strong feelings, and loves to run full tilt. That's my Shannon, and she'll always have my heart. I guess I would be scared if that's not what I wanted, but I like the intensity and fire of what we have. I fell in love with it before she was mine."

T.J.'s truth touched Cooper, but he didn't tell his face. He agreed with the headrest in front of him and let T.J. go back to eating peanuts and examining clouds.

LIBBY WAS WAITING for him at the baggage carousel. She didn't bring the kids, which surprised him. Then he noticed the dark circles under her eyes and her puffy eyelids. She'd put on makeup, but lines marred her normally smooth, flawless forehead and the corners of her mouth. Or maybe he was just now observing the natural aging process.

She looked tired. He gave her a big hug and felt her melt into him, draw strength from his shoulders, allowing him to hold her in standing position as if her legs couldn't support her.

He brushed the hair from her face and pressed his palms against her cheeks. Instantly, her eyes teared up.

A jolt of apprehension shot down his spine all the way to his toes. His first thought was about the kids, and he hoped something wasn't wrong with one of them.

"What is it?"

"My mom is scheduled for surgery tomorrow morning. She has breast cancer. She had a biopsy without telling anyone until she got the results. They have to remove both breasts."

"Oh, honey. I'm so sorry. How's she feeling?"

"She looks great. Says she feels fine, but she's scared. I can tell she's worried, and that worries me too."

"How's your dad taking it?"

"He's on a trip. He gets back later in the week. She hasn't wanted to tell him on the phone."

"But it's surgery—"

"I know, but that's not what she wants to do. She wants to tell him when she's in recovery. I mean, I see her point. And I know he'll be pissed when he learns what's happened."

"Hell, yeah. I would be. You can't at least talk her into giving him a call tonight? He'd cancel anything to come home and be with her."

"Coop, he wouldn't get here in time anyway. He's in Japan giving a talk. It's what he loves to do. She doesn't want to take that away from him."

Coop knew better than to try to convince either of the most important women in his life to change their mind. He was going to have to go with the flow. He could do that.

He had ice water in his veins. T.J. had just confirmed it.

CHAPTER 2

CARLA BROWNLEE HAD cookbooks and magazines spread all over her bed, which was unmade. She'd showered, dressed, and was just putting on her earrings and lipstick when Libby entered their master suite.

"What's all this?" she asked her mother.

"I'm going to beat this, Libby. I've made up my mind. I'm going to learn all the new methods they have now for beating cancer. You know there is a nearly eighty-nine percent survival rate? And breast cancer is one of the easiest to cure."

Libby liked that her mother was so positive and was taking control over her treatment and future health. It was how she approached everything in life. She wondered how it would feel to have the huge scars on her chest instead of her soft breasts and felt a tinge of remorse she had the gall to complain to friends she wasn't as round as before.

Her mom was going on about herbal remedies. Libby made a note to ask Coop for some backup information. "Are you listening to me?"

"I am. Sorry. I was just thinking about Grandma. Wasn't it cancer?"

"She had it at a much younger age. But yes."

"Which means I should be checked. That test they are having girls get these days."

"BRCA test. It's a gene test for mutations. You should ask your doctor about it, Libby."

Carla finished in the bathroom and stepped out into the bedroom like she was stepping on stage. Today, in person, she didn't appear to be nervous. Last night on the phone had worried Libby.

"Okay, are you ready?"

Libby was making the bed.

"Don't bother with that. I'm having Ynez coming to clean this afternoon, and she'll change the sheets. I want to come home to everything clean."

They scampered downstairs. Carla checked her rose garden in the backyard, sprinkling some water at the base of the bushes. They were just beginning to bloom. The grounds were immaculate, forming a natural border around the pool area and lawn beyond. It took a crew of three on a weekly basis to keep it looking so nice. They even weeded her mother's raised beds when she didn't get to it. Her flowers won ribbons at the San Diego County Fair every year, especially her dahlias and roses.

"It looks stunning, Mom. I think the prettiest I've ever seen it."

Carla stopped beside her, long enough to scan the yard one last time, and agree with her daughter. "I'll be taking out a lot of the flowers in the beds so I can grow my own vegetables. Broccoli and cabbage. As soon as I feel up to it, I'm going to get starts from the nursery. Juicing is supposed to be good."

"Go slow, Mom. Take it easy and pace yourself."

"Oh, don't be ridiculous, Libby. Gardening relaxes me. Not like the old days when I had to bend over and work rows. I hated the weeding. But these raised beds make light work of it."

"But you don't want to over-do. That won't be good."

"I intend to surprise everyone with how fast I heal. Like I said, I'm going to beat this thing. It's war."

They locked the kitchen and back side doors, made sure the other windows were locked, and then exited out the front door. The Brownlee's had one of the Spanish Revival houses with black iron grates over the windows and decorative awnings. The front door was hand-carved and came from Mexico on one of their diving trips.

On the way to the surgery center, she asked about whether or not her mom had called her brother, Neil.

"Oh, Heaven's no. Neil has his own issues. Last time I talked to him he said his household was drowning in women. That's all he would need. And first thing he'd do is call Austin and shame him into coming home."

"It's your life, Mom. But I hope you're prepared for the fallout when they find out they were kept in the dark. You know Dad especially will feel it."

"Libby, I'm just having two pieces of flesh removed from my chest. That's it. I'm going to have them do it so I can get a nice boob job after I heal. I've wanted it ever since you were born. They can do that, you know. They create an extra flap of skin so later on they can do reconstructive work. It's just amazing what they can accomplish these days."

Her mother's attitude almost resembled someone looking forward to the surgery, instead of it being a medical emergency. Carla kept prattling on about her research, about people she knew who had fully recovered. This was clearly going to put her back a few paces, but Libby drew strength from her mother's confidence in the outcome.

"Can I call Dad and Neil and let them know after you're safely out of surgery?"

"Let's wait a day. They do tests while they have me under. Let's get the results first, and then we'll call them."

"Okay, but do any of your friends know about this?" With their circle of friends, Libby could imagine word getting out ahead of her call to her dad.

"Not a word. This all happened so fast anyway. I didn't tell anyone I was having the biopsy."

"I did tell Coop. He's my support system. I didn't tell the kids, though."

"That's fine." Carla sat with her hands neatly folded in her lap, her overnight bag perched on her lap as if Libby was taking her to a sleepover like she occasionally did for her daughter, Gillian.

"Are you in any pain?" she asked.

"No. A little tender in the nipple area, where it's inverted. I think that's where the bulk of the mass is. If I squeeze, it's tender. But honestly, I don't feel sick at all."

"Hold that thought. I'm sure you'll feel like you got your lights punched out when you get out of surgery, but you're probably right. You'll bounce right back in no time."

Carla ignored her statement and asked about the kids.

"They're both in school, but I have Luci Begay picking them up afterward. Depending on how long you're in recovery, I might let them stay over."

"That's a good idea. Besides, Coop is now home so that will give you a night to yourselves. How was his trip?"

"He said he learned a lot. But he's glad to be home."

"Who did he go with?"

"T.J. Talbot."

"The troublemaker!"

"He's not a troublemaker, Mom. That's in his past. Coop really enjoys his company."

"I hope T.J. doesn't encourage him to drink."

"That's a long time ago. You know this." Libby was beginning to get annoyed with the extra hovering her mother was doing. It was an act, she thought, pretending to be in control when in actuality there wasn't any such thing.

You don't fool me, Mom. You're nervous as hell.

She parked in the surgery patient parking lot close to the front entrance. Carla made it through the double automatic doors before Libby was halfway from the car to the entrance.

Her mother showed her where to sign in, below Carla's name, and then she plastered a visitor badge on her shirt. "There you go. All official." She smiled up at Libby for the first time. "This is my patient number so you can track me on the monitors. They'll be calling me any minute, but they're running a few minutes behind. You don't really have to wait. I can take it from here."

That flipped a switch. "Mom, stop it!" She placed her

hands on Carla Brownlee's upper arms and lightly gripped her. "I'm here to be your moral support today. I wouldn't even think of abandoning you here. You think I could drop you off and go shopping or something? Come on, give me a little credit."

"It's not that big a deal," her mother stubbornly insisted.

"No, you're wrong. It *is* a big deal. You've got to stop being so prickly. Let someone help *you* for a change."

Her mother relaxed her shoulders and pretended to sigh. "Oh, all right. I guess I'm being impatient and can't wait for all this to be over."

Libby had always maintained a closer relationship with her father because of the dynamics now rearing their ugly head between them. She had studied counseling, as her father was a renowned psychiatrist who was in great demand for speaking and television or radio jobs. One of his specialties was working with some of the SEALs who came home with severe cases of PTSD and was considered an authority on it.

But Libby wasn't looking forward to the conversation she'd have with him soon. He would naturally feel he'd been left out of the decision making. She would argue the point but didn't want to stress her mother any further. So, for now, she acquiesced, knowing there would come a day she'd regret that decision.

Her mother's driver personality made it difficult for Libby to show affection toward her, as if she was being stiff-armed, held at bay. But again, she went along with it, for now.

"Let us take care of you, Mom. Let's not go any faster than we need to. This isn't a sprint. We don't want to overlook anything. You need to stay calm."

Carla Brownlee removed herself from Libby's embrace and sat in a waiting room chair, staring up at a computer screen with patient numbers on it followed by color-coded comments. Libby saw her mother's number listed as checked in. A few minutes later, they were called inside the surgery reception area. Libby was asked to wait until her mother's clothes and personal effects could be gathered up.

Carla fussed with something but refused help until one of the nurses slipped behind the curtain and helped her with it. Then the drape was pulled away, revealing her mother looking small, not elegantly dressed, and hooked up to a heart monitor and an I.V. She had on a blue gown that was tied in front.

"Did you bring your cell, Mom?"

"It's in my purse."

"You sure you don't want to call Dad? Last chance."

"Nope. Made up my mind and not changing it. You and I will talk to the doctor first."

"Okay."

"Is Coop coming over later?"

"Maybe. Depends."

"You should have him here for you."

The comment stung a bit. Her mother refused to drop the attitude. But, like the rest of her life, Carla Brownlee was going to do this as close to one hundred percent *her* way as possible.

The surgeon dropped by to explain the procedures. Carla interrupted him and indicated she'd already had it explained to her. She was ready.

"Do you have any questions, Libby?" he asked her.

"How long will it be?"

"It will be about three hours before you can see her if everything goes according to plan. That's not a three-hour surgery, but it takes nearly an hour in the recover room. And we have to wait for a bed on the surgery floor sometimes. So don't worry if it takes longer than that. Will you be staying in the waiting room?"

"I was planning on it."

"You can take off for an hour, maybe two. It will be that long before I can come out. So go do some errands. I'll bet you haven't had breakfast yet."

"You're exactly right."

"Go have a good meal. Go home, put your feet up for a bit. Then come back. I'll see you around ten or so, okay?"

"Thanks, doctor."

"See, I told you. Just go, Libby," her mother added.

"Well, it's natural she wants to wait until you're in surgery, Carla. Don't be too hard on her. Waiting is very stressful sometimes. She's doing you a favor by coming. Don't be stubborn."

Carla Brownlee's eyes got huge. Libby knew she was slightly offended.

"Good luck with that, Dr. Green. My dad's been working on that for over thirty-five years. He'll be pleased if you can cure that, too, along with the cancer."

Dr. Green chuckled. "Is Austin coming by later on?"

"No. He's in Japan at a conference. I'm afraid she didn't want us to call him."

Libby's mother crossed her arms and stared daggers back

at her. "Libby! Stop that nonsense." She addressed the doctor. "I knew he'd cancel his trip. He's getting an award, and he's the keynote speaker. He was so looking forward to this. I didn't want to take that away from him."

"It was the right choice to go in there right away, but you should have told him at least." He sighed. "Okay, ladies, I need to get prepped. See you in a couple of hours, Libby. She's going to do fine. If she wakes up early, I promise to not let her grab the scalpel and complete the surgery herself."

"That would be a good thing, Doctor."

He walked away, chuckling to himself. Her mother pursed her lips.

"Dr. Green has a horrible bedside manner. I'm going to put that on Yelp when I get out of here and get back on my computer."

Libby was certain she would do just that. It would probably be the first thing she did when she came home.

CHAPTER 3

THE IRON WAS flying at Gunny's Gym as S.O. Calvin Cooper met up with Fredo and Kyle Lansdowne for an hour-long workout. Former Chief Petty Officer Timmons, who had married Amornpan Wattanapanit, Gunny's widow, was behind the counter, folding tee shirts in the display case and wiping down the mirrors behind him.

"Watch it. You're gonna break my floor!" Timmons barked in his raspy, unhealthy voice to Lt. Malcolm Jones, former member of Kyle's squad, but now attached to SEAL Team 5. Jones was designated the new heavy lifter king by a wide margin. His shoulders looked like bowling balls, Coop observed.

That kind of workout required that he drop the massive weights, and even though the gym was floored with specialized rubber shock-absorbing material that smelled of tires, wall to wall, it still sounded like metal on concrete. It also resembled the vibration a large fast-moving truck would make cruising past the little conclave.

Coop thought that someday, when they got ready to replace the rubber mats, they would indeed find shatter cracks in the concrete floor from all the tossing Jones did.

"That's part of it, Timmons. Don't ruin my fun," Jones spouted back. He wiped down the bench he'd been sitting on, which was nearly dripping with sweat.

"You can drop them. Just don't throw them," Timmons corrected.

"Ladies, ladies, can't we all get along?" barked Kyle Lansdown. "And, Jones, you get any bigger, you'll have to invest in another four-hundred-dollar uniform."

"I'm out, Kyle. Got four months to go. Might be able to skip the next rotation."

Coop thought he could add fuel to the fire with his good idea. "Why don't you brace that dump with your foot, that way you can turn your big toe into pudding, get out on a medical, and get a disability pension for life?"

"He can't," interrupted Fredo. "He can't stand the sight of blood. Right, Jones?"

"You guys are lucky none of my besties are in here from Team 5," quipped Jones.

"What do you mean 'besties'? They all took up a collection to get rid of you. I heard the rumors," said Kyle.

"See, that's why I hang with Team 5. They got lots more respect for this brother. Besides which, they're bigger guys. All of them. You guys have the Smurf crew on Team 3. Although, Fredo, you look like you growed a couple of inches. I guess having twins has that effect on you, right?"

"Jones, you best not go there. He can still out climb you. I think he's faster in the sprint too," added Cooper.

"And you don't want to wrestle him, because of the dipstick thing," T.J. added.

Fredo was known for putting a finger on a guy's ass to get enough of a reaction he could complete a takedown, if the guy wasn't expecting it, of course. It was cheating, but few opponents would call him out for it out of embarrassment.

The huge SEAL from Team 5 wet his towel and slapped it across Fredo's butt. "We'll have to test that theory one fine day, Fredo. Until then, gents, hang it loose." When Malcolm Jones left the room, it suddenly felt like a ballroom instead of a bunker.

"Why do some guys have to get so big?" T.J. swore. "It doesn't do anything for you performance-wise."

"I think he's looking for a Mrs. Jones," said Fredo. "He was dating one of Mia's friends, and she dumped him hard. Like those bars. Can you believe he's what thirty-five and never been married?"

"Admiral Coe was forty-seven when he got married," said Kyle.

"But he already had four kids," said Coop. "Maybe he's worried he'll die a spinster."

"The way he throws things around, he probably can't work out at more than a handful of places with concrete floors. Old buildings." Timmons continued spraying and wiping down the benches and the equipment.

"He's a vintage one-of-a-kind, that one," said Cooper.

"Pee-you!" Danny Begay was at the door. "Someone has a glandular problem." He held his nose.

"Jones just left, and he was throwing his bars and raining sweat everywhere. You be careful, because it's damned slippery here today," said Timmons.

Danny worked in a routine with T.J. so they could spot each other.

Coop's phone rang. He knew it must be Libby.

"Now that's a fine, Cooper. We don't bring our cell phones in here," said Timmons.

"Libby's mom is in for surgery this morning. I gotta take the call." He stepped outside.

At first, he couldn't hear, due to the traffic now flowing past the strip of downtown Coronado.

"Honey, is everything okay? You're gonna have to speak up a little. Can't hear you."

"I'm just checking in. Can you hear me now?"

"Yup. So she's in surgery? Did you talk to the doctor?"

"Won't be for another hour or two. I was going to see if you wanted to have breakfast with me, or do you have a ways to go?"

"No, I can be available in about twenty. Of course, I'm not smelling very nice."

"I like the way you smell, Coop. I always do. Why don't we stay casual, go to the Scupper? I'm feeling like a crab omelet."

"Okay. You have the kids covered, or do you need me—"

"Luci Begay said she'd pick them up. I was hoping you'd stop by the hospital this afternoon, maybe talk to Mom."

"Sure. I was planning on that. Look, I'll meet up with you in about thirty minutes, okay? We can talk over breakfast."

"Sounds good. See you."

Cooper headed back into the gym and began using one of the leg press machines. Kyle came over.

"How was North Carolina? T.J. said it was a full class."

"Packed. Never seen it so full. Of course, they are training some border guard EMTs too. Can you believe it, emergency medical aid at the border? They have to be ready just like we're at war," Coop answered.

"It's a war all right," mumbled Kyle. "Can't let the women and kids die on us. We don't do that here."

"Agreed. I can't remember going for the cert with so much discussion on drugs, overdoses, and mental illness. Don't get me wrong, it's needed, and always has been, but man, we must be racking up the stats to have them so worried about it. We went over warning signs, reactions to some of the new drugs coming in. The drug cartels are working overtime these days. And our instructor said they're targeting the military, because they now recruit from there with all the weapons training."

"That's a frightful thought. But it's been that way now for years. They target misfits, people who don't fit in. They make the best recruits, and they'll do just about anything to get their hands on drugs. A big danger, and the Headshed is nervous about it."

"As they should be. It's pouring in. They get off with the courts being so overloaded."

"Making hay while they can. Open season, I guess. I'm sure glad that's not my job," Kyle said. "I feel sorry for those guys and what they see every day now."

"We talked a little with some of those guys. Lots of civilian volunteers down there too. It's really not safe for that kind of program," said Coop.

"We're getting some orders coming through soon. I have a

feeling it's back to Baja again. We had a top-level discussion about volunteers either being on the inside with cartels or innocents getting in the way. Either way, it's a sorry situation and not improving, either."

"Soon?"

"I think so."

Cooper wasn't looking forward to going back to Baja California. They'd barely had three months since their last deployment.

"So how's Libby's mom?" Kyle finally asked.

"Libby hasn't talked to the doctor yet. She's still in surgery."

"May I ask what for?"

"She just got diagnosed with breast cancer. She's having a double mastectomy this morning."

"I'm sorry, Coop. Give her my best. How's Austin doing? I'm sure he's all over the surgeon."

"He's in Japan at a conference. She didn't tell him. Can you believe that?"

"Maybe it's not as serious as it sounds. Some women have the surgery as a preventative."

"No, Kyle. She had biopsies on both sides, and both were fully invaded. I am holding my breath. I'm meeting Libby in a bit, and this afternoon, I want to be there when the doc gives his prognosis. Fingers crossed they get everything."

"Well, best of luck with that. Christy and I will be praying for her. When does Austin get back?"

"Not for another three days. By that time, she should be resting at home."

"Does she have help?"

"I'm pretty sure they've arranged that already. With the kids, Libby can't wait on her twenty-four seven."

"And probably not a good idea either. You should have her talk to Christy. She lost her mother the very same way. In fact, that's how she got down here. Her mother left her the condo. She'd just gotten her license. In a way, I owe my whole life to her mom."

"I never took you for a Pollyanna, Kyle."

"Ah, shucks. You guys are rubbing off on me."

LIBBY WAS ALREADY seated when Coop arrived at the Scupper. He slipped in behind her, gave her a backwards hug and several kisses on her neck at her hairline, then took a seat.

"How are you holding up?"

Libby's face was pale. The early morning rise to get her mom to the center by seven-thirty had deprived her of some restful sleep. He knew for certain she didn't get much last night, and he was responsible for that too.

Her eyes immediately filled with water.

"Hey, what's going on, sweetheart?" He moved to sit next to her instead of across the table.

"She's pushing me away, bossing me around like I'm ten or something. I really don't like when she gets this way. Except now she's sick, and I can't argue or push back."

"Well, that won't turn out well. Trust me, Carla's using it to full advantage knowing that. You should just be honest with her. Or are you not sure you're thinking straight?"

"Well, she has this positive attitude, but she's overcompensating. Talking about planting a vegetable garden and starting to juice, study herbs and such. She's convinced she'll lick this cancer and that it's no problem."

"Well, that's okay, until there *is* a problem. And that's when you have to be there for her. Hey, if she can think her way into being healthy again after the surgery, more power to her." He took her hand, extending his arm over her shoulders with the other. "What's really bothering you?"

Libby stared out through the window, studying the sailboats and the stacks of unused crab nets. With that still faraway look, she answered him. "When does it start to get easier, Coop? I'm uncomfortable with her not wanting me to tell Dad. I know he's going to be upset with me for not overruling her."

"But she has a lot on her plate with the surgery. You can surely cut her a little slack."

"So why, then, doesn't she want her full support system in place? I'm only one piece of it. Am I wrong? I feel kind of resentful. That's going to be an unpleasant conversation."

"You're siding with your dad on this. I understand that. You two are very close. Probably feels like a low-level betrayal."

"Exactly!"

"Who has she told?"

"No one. I'm not surprised she hasn't called Neil. That will be my job. I'll get grilled for it, but I can handle that. It's my dad I feel bad about."

"Go home, Libby. Get some rest. I think that's what you need, although I appreciate the invite for breakfast. I think you should just go to bed. I'll come home and get you when it's time to go back to the hospital. Her doctor said a couple of hours?"

Libby nodded.

"Whatever the news is, Libby, you'll handle it much better if you get some rest. Trust me. We had it pounded into us over the last couple of weeks. Better than any medication. Rest. Restorative sleep. That's what you need. I shouldn't have been so selfish with you last night."

"No, I wanted that too. I needed that."

Cooper scanned her sad eyes, drifting down to her soft, ample lips. That's when he realized he *didn't* have ice water in his veins. That had all been some of T.J.'s B.S.

He loved and wanted to protect her. Her concern and pain were spilling all over him too. He wished he could take some of that burden away, but the only thing left to do was let her know how precious she was to him.

He wondered if he should make the comment he was compelled to make. Then he decided to do it.

"Thing is, sweetheart, the way you are with me and with the kids, that's another kind of mothering. You'd never do that to us, would you?"

She shook her head and let the tears fall down her cheeks.

"It's just the way she is. She's a driver, Libby. When she's under pressure, she goes straight to her wheel well. She becomes focused on one thing at a time, and right now, she wants to get rid of the obstacle to her long life. It doesn't have anything to do with you, except if you interfere with what she wants."

He was heartened that she was agreeing with him or agreeing to agree with him—putting up the pretense anyway. He knew it was hard for her not to let her feelings get hurt. She was under stress as well, after all.

"That tornado took all my relatives away in just a few minutes. I had to grieve for all of them at once. I told myself I wasn't going to cry, but in the end, that's all I could do. And I had the Brotherhood behind me. Kyle and everyone were super. And they're there for you too. Together, we'll all get through this."

He hugged her when she stood, watching her shapely body exit the Scupper. Her hips had that sway of a confident wife, mother, and daughter. She hadn't experienced as much loss in her life as Cooper had. There was the tragedy of Madame M, her former employer in San Francisco, but nothing had taken away her family unit like Coop's was taken away that day in one of the largest and most deadly tornadoes in Nebraska recorded history.

The bright Coronado sun hit her face, the gentle mid-day wind blowing her long auburn hair in the breeze, almost looking like it was on fire. She was statuesque, just like her mother and just as strong, made of pure female stock with all the best parts in ample supply. She had intuition, her heart was kind, and she didn't like being shut out, chased, or ignored.

She was far more similar to her mother than she could possibly know. But some of their differences were glaring, depending on the area. That was about to be tested, Coop realized.

She didn't look back at him sitting in the dark watching her walk into the light. She placed her sunglasses carefully on the bridge of her nose, inhaled, and set her course.

And then she was gone.

Now he knew how Austin Brownlee, Libby's dad, would feel if the unimaginable were to occur with Carla. Even in the old familiar haunt like the Scupper, where the lights were low because it was going to be a hot afternoon, he suddenly felt all alone. And very sad.

He saw remnants of his family farm, the tractor on its side, the large rear wheel still turning in the wind. Nothing was left of their barn, their dairy goats, or the house. The tornado had made a bloody gash in the land and swallowed them all up in it.

Then and now, he sat in the dark, hoping that he could help the most important person in his life cope with something she'd never thought about before.

The mortality of life and how little any of them had control over it.

CHAPTER 4

LIBBY ALMOST DROPPED by the kids' school just so she could smell the sweetness of her children. Will, her oldest—named after her deceased uncle, Austin Brownlee's twin brother, who perished as a Special Operator while on a mission in Grenada—would instantly pick up something wasn't right with his mother. For that reason alone, she decided to do what she'd promised: go home and take a nap.

But she wanted to hug him and smell his prepubescent little-man scent. Even his child sweat was like perfume to her. She'd be able to tell her kids from others blindfolded. She knew the sound of their breathing when they slept. Gillian's stubbornness was just like her grandmother's. Her daughter was built like a young giraffe, all legs, knees, and ankles with a tall, skinny frame just like Coop.

She missed them both but didn't want to impose on their normal life at school. There would be time to explain Grandma's surgery later. Libby had no doubt her mother would even show them the scars. Maybe Libby would have to step in and stop that since it might frighten them.

Their bungalow was only a few blocks to the beach. Normally, that would be enough to soothe anything that was troubling her. Today, she needed sleep.

The stucco single-story house had an attractive white picket fence out front with an iron gate beneath an expansive yellow rose trellis in full bloom. She parked in front of their single-car garage, leaving enough space for Coop's Hummer when he arrived later on.

She entered the house through the kitchen at the rear. The traffic on these little side beach streets was minimal, so she listened and could hear the roar of the ocean and the waves hitting the firm sand.

She shed her clothes and left her lacy white underwear on, slipping into the cool sheets of their California King bed. The extra length was not enough for Coop's tall frame, but most of the time, they slept together in each other's arms, their legs and arms tangled deliciously.

She listened to the sounds of the ocean again through her open bedroom window until she faded into a deep sleep.

LIBBY AWOKE TO the feel of Coop's hand on her belly, slowly making its way up to her breasts and slipping under her bra. His deft fingers massaged the hook loose, and she was freed at last. She opened her eyes and saw his warm smile, asking for permission he really didn't have to have. She hoped it would always be this way between the two of them.

She began slipping her panties down her hips while he helped. Her bare pubic area pressed against his thigh, riding him deliciously, the flesh-on-flesh experience making her wet.

Before long, she was arching to receive him as he held her

upper body, his long arms slipping beneath her and his hands gripping her shoulders. He lifted her gently, kissed her lips slowly, tugged at her bottom lip with his teeth, and then moaned as he entered her, watching her face. He was soon lost in the rhythm of the song their two bodies played.

She quickly wrapped her legs around his hips and indulged in the goodness of being loved by this Adonis, the gentle giant of a man with the strength of a hundred. The man who gave her their two children, the man who would always be there for her.

She became urgent, and he answered her intensity with each stroke, bringing her to the edge of reality.

Their hot and sweaty lovemaking left her breathless afterwards. It had smoothed her insides and calmed her soul. His gentle nibbles afterward told her he was her devoted servant, that she could lean on him as much as she needed to. She was filled with gratitude.

"God, Coop, you make me feel like I'm twenty again. Our sex life has only gotten better with age."

"Of course," he said, planting a soft kiss on her lips. "Practice makes perfect, sweetheart. I love exploring all the ways I can make you come."

She rolled her head to the side, and he lovingly kissed her neck, letting his fingers sift through her hair. Whenever he talked in bed like this, she felt the warm vibration of his voice throughout his upper torso as they pressed against each other. Her body needed more, but there wasn't time.

He lifted her naked out of the bed, presented her to the shower, and turned the water on, pushing her into the cold stream and making her scream with delight. He held her there until the water began to warm, and they took turns lathering each other with the herbal shower gel he loved. His fingers shampooed her hair patiently, making her ears buzz with the firmness of his rubbing motion.

Still slippery from shampoo and soap, he turned her around and pressed her against the now warming tiles of the shower wall. He lifted her buttocks and spread them in his enormous hands and placed himself at her opening from behind. She gasped at the quick entry, the way he stretched her. She was putty in his hands, lifted by his stroke so expertly delivered. He spanked her bottom as he sunk into her deeper with each long hip movement. One hand moved down to touch her bud. He was relentless with his demand she surrender to him, and finally, he begged her to come.

It had been a stolen few minutes of pleasure that came all too infrequently for them, since their days were spent around the kids' activities, Coop's work, and Libby's occasional clients at her dad's luxurious psychiatric offices. And maybe that's why she enjoyed it so much this morning.

She'd missed this.

Dressed and holding hands, they took the EV Hummer to the surgery center at the hospital. Coop brought two water bottles for both of them, but once she set foot inside the lobby area, she couldn't drink the cold liquid. She wanted coffee, so he went in search of some.

While Coop was off with his errand, Libby checked the computer screen and saw her mother's number go from Red to Blue, indicating she was awake and in the recovery room. She pointed it out to Coop when he returned with her latte.

They sat side-by-side, their thighs touching from their knees to hips, their hands clasped, resting on Libby's leg. He was studying the motion his thumb made over her knuckles.

"That was nice, Libby. I have to say that was one of my favorites," he whispered, staring deep into her eyes and making her blush.

Someone in the waiting room coughed, but she didn't look away. "It was, Coop. I'm available tonight if you still have time."

Their lips touched, their tongues connected, and the delicious fire in her belly sent juices to her panties. "Where do I sign up?" he answered.

She couldn't help herself and giggled.

"Ah, that's what I like to hear. I've missed your laugh," he said.

When they parted, several others in the waiting room looked away quickly.

"I think we put on a little show, Libby," he muttered under his breath, studying their audience.

"Love on full display. I'm not afraid of a little harmless kissing. Daring to go further."

"Mrs. Cooper, your husband must be the luckiest man on the planet," Coop whispered.

"Mmhmm. He's got wicked skills."

"And he's trained you well, too, I'll bet."

She angled her head and covered her mouth in a little titter. "You're making me blush, Coop."

He leaned into her, kissed her ear, and whispered, "And

you're making me hard."

She squeezed his fingers just as Dr. Green presented himself to them.

"If I could bother you two for a couple of minutes. I have an update." He was clearly not in a very pleasant mood.

Libby was embarrassed at the inappropriateness of their behavior. An older woman whispered something to the gentleman sitting next to her. Coop stood and helped her up before shaking Dr. Green's hand.

"Let's take a little walk down the hallway." Dr. Green led the way out of the waiting area.

Libby began to feel anxious in the pit of her stomach. By the way Coop clutched her hand, she could tell he was nervous too.

"How did she do, Doctor?" Libby asked.

"She tolerated the surgery. She's a good, healthy, strong woman, and she's a fighter." He sighed, scanning the polished vinyl flooring of the hall area. "And she's going to need every bit of that strength."

Libby's first reaction was to put her hand over her mouth. Her eyes began to sting and then water.

"How so, Dr. Green?" asked Coop.

"We removed all of the tissue we could. I'm concerned we didn't get it all, so we'll have to wait for the lab results, and that should be sometime tonight. I'd recommend waiting until we get those before we discuss anything with her as far as her options."

"Options? What do you mean *options?*"

"The type of cancer she has is very aggressive, and it had

invaded much more than we suspected. I had to remove the lymph nodes under both her arms because they all looked involved, or probably were involved, due to the size and scope of the cancer. And it came dangerously close to her rib cage. We normally don't like to see it attaching to bone, because then, well, we have a much more serious problem."

Libby began to lean against Coop, and he adjusted himself, one arm clasped around her body to hold her steady. Her face felt cold and clammy. She began to sweat but not from overheating. She was scared. She'd never been so scared.

"Is this survivable?" she finally asked.

"Oh, yes, people do survive. All the time these days. But it's a real shame she waited so long to get checked. So I'm going to tell you straight, like I told Austin—"

"You called my dad?" Libby gasped.

"Of course I did. He'd have done the same for me. I wanted him to hear it from my lips to his ears, since we're friends and have been for many years."

"She told me not to say anything to him until she got home and was recovering."

"Well, that's the thing. She may need further surgery. We're going to do a scan and see if there are any invasions elsewhere. Then we'll come up with a plan. Austin said he'd be catching a flight out early tomorrow morning."

"But his speech—"

"Has been cancelled, Libby. You know better than that."

"But Mom—"

The doctor looked back and forth between the two of them. "You two are going to have to help her accept the reality of her situation. If she does survive, there's a lot of pretty heavy treatment coming her way. I won't lie to you. It's going to be brutal if she wants to tackle it aggressively. And I think she will. Austin said the same."

"But at some point, the cure is worse than the disease, doctor. Isn't that right?" Coop commented.

"Well, in this case, sure. Yet without the cure, Carla won't last more than a few months. We think we got everything, but because it invaded both sets of lymph nodes, I mean fully invaded, it's more than likely already spread, and we just can't see it yet. So we'll be designing a cocktail for her, maybe some radiation treatment. One good thing about Carla is that she's stubborn. She's going to need to be stubborn to accept all this."

Libby began to weep but didn't make a sound. Tears gushed from her eyes, and soon, she was gasping for breath.

"I'd go home, Libby, if I were you. She gets a good look at your face and you'll scare her. We have to wait until later on tonight to hear about the lab results. Try to remain calm. Tell her I've been wishy-washy. My patients tell me that all the time anyway. But will you please tell her I called Austin, and he wants a call from her whenever she feels like it? Tonight, if possible."

"What time is it there?"

"I woke him up. Even late tonight would work, since he's beginning his morning now. He can't get out until tomorrow, but he's working on that. You can blame it all on me if you have to."

"Was he angry?" Libby asked.

Dr. Green put his hand on her shoulder and smirked.

"Disappointed is the word I'd use. But I think he understands. I knew he would have to be told, since this wasn't a benign tumor or anything. And he'd be even more angry the longer he had to wait for the news."

"So when can we see her, Doc?" asked Cooper.

"I'll have the recovery nurse come get you when she's ready. Be prepared to be peppered with questions. She was already asking them as she regained consciousness. She won't remember that at all, but I had to tell her to be patient. She nearly threw a pillow at me."

Dr. Green and Cooper shared a chuckle that Libby didn't find amusing at all.

"Well, I've got other patients to talk to. I sure did hope that it would be better news. She's got a great oncologist who really knows his stuff and is up to date on the latest treatments. She's in good hands."

"Will we see you tonight then?" Libby asked.

"I hope so. But if it's after dinner and we don't have anything back, then it won't be until tomorrow. I've told the nurse this, but you can reassure Carla she'll hear as soon as I do, okay?"

"Yessir. Thanks for your expert hands," Coop said as they shook again.

"Thank you. And, Libby?" he said as he took Libby's hands in both of his, "I hate this part of things, the waiting. But once we know who the enemy is, we can set up a plan to wipe him out. Coop here can relate to that, I'm guessing."

"Yessir. Makes perfect sense. We won't worry until we have to."

"Exactly. Okay, I'm off to make some happier calls. I needed to get this one done first. Frankly, it ruined my day, but I never give up. Providence shines down on those who expect miracles, so we'll concentrate on that, okay?"

"Thank you, Dr. Green." It was all she could do to utter just that.

Coop was leading her over to the waiting area.

"No, I don't want to go back there."

CHAPTER 5

COOP BROUGHT LIBBY outside so they could get some air and have a private chat. It wasn't as hot as it was going to be later on in the day. He was concerned because Libby hadn't had anything but coffee. Even with the nap and magical lovemaking, she was burning up her energy pennies faster than she could create them.

Her steps were plodding, moving zombie-like, so he took care in guiding her tenderly into the tiny rose garden built off the chapel where he knew there was a cool concrete bench. Some couple had donated a small angel waterfall, which stood in the corner of the garden, continuously flowing like an eternal flame. She seemed to relax, no longer digging her fingernails into the back of his hand.

"Honey, you should get something in your stomach."

"I'm not hungry. I can't eat when I'm like this." And then she collapsed into his chest. "Oh, Coop, my poor mother. Carved up like a totem. All that pain ahead of her. And maybe no cure."

"You heard the doctor. He said lots of people survive this. You need a thimbleful of your mother's courage. You normally have that."

"This is different. I wasn't expecting this."

Coop held her while she cried. He rubbed her back and thought about how many men he'd held while their life slipped into the ether. He used to wonder about it when he began his medic training, what it would feel like to hold someone, to guide them on their way. And then when it happened to him the first time, he was changed. He began to look for clues of an afterlife. But everyone's process was both slightly different and chillingly the same. Some people he knew well, like his team buddies. Others—villagers and innocent civilians caught in the crossfire of war—were strangers he sent on their way as if they were relatives. Because that's what they deserved.

He'd seen more of death than he wanted. He considered himself one of the lucky ones because someone had to be able to deal with it, so others didn't have to. But it was harder this time, with Libby's mom. The death, if that was the outcome, affected someone he loved. His children's grandmother. The woman who had given birth to Libby and kept Austin's heart on fire. Only thing to do was be prepared for anything and be grateful for every minute, because that's what he could control.

They stared at the bubbling water and the evidence of the kindness of man, that the parents could reach out and make an impact on someone else's in their grief. That was the best and the most horrible part of these gateway moments, he thought.

He brushed the hair from her face, and he saw she was beginning to unfreeze. He kissed her forehead. "Come on. Let's get you some soup, okay?"

She nodded.

Upstairs in the cafeteria, they had two hearty pots of steaming deliciousness. One was baked potato-bacon, and the other was golden mushroom. Coop knew she'd want the mushroom. He bought a slice of cornbread to go along with it. They sat beside a large picture window overlooking the parking lot and let the warm liquid cheer them up. He watched her devour the cornbread and slurp every drop of soup, finishing it before he did.

She sat back, satisfied. Smiling once again, she said, "Good idea, Cooper. I just might make it the rest of the day without bursting into tears."

He held her hands in his, her fingers still chilled to the touch but getting warmer.

"Are you ready?"

"As good as I'll ever be. Thanks for the suggestion. As usual, you know exactly what I need."

Yeah, T.J. was full of shit. He didn't have ice water in his veins. Next time he tried to tell him that, he'd pay for his crime.

WHEN THEY RETURNED to the waiting area, a nurse in scrubs and facemask greeted them. "You want to see your mom now?" she asked with a cheerful smile.

"Sure. How's she doing?"

"I think she did real good. She's not in pain right now, but she has drains and tubing everywhere, and I know she's feeling stiff, which is what the anesthetic does to a person." She pushed open double swinging doors.

The room was painted a light blue with lots of artwork on

the walls, some of it done by children. Coop guessed these had all been donated by patients who had come before. Someone was in pain and asking for help in an incessant whine like a screen door flapping back and forth in the wind. It was an elderly person, from the sounds of the voice. Someone who shouldn't be left alone.

The nurse pulled aside a flowered curtain, and there was Carla, her face a little swollen but otherwise of good color. She'd even managed to get lipstick on her. She never went anywhere without her red lipstick.

"Hey there, beautiful. Wanna dance?" he said to her.

"Oh, Coop. You lie miserably. I thought you said this was a health spa. They stole my boobs," she said, pointing below her chin. Other than the mass of bandages beneath her sheet, her chest was completely flat. She'd always been amble in that department, like her lovely daughter.

Libby smiled through her tears, leaning over to give her a kiss on the cheek. "Hi, Mom. He is right. You look great."

"You'd think I could get a nice massage with some lavender-scented oil. But no, I'm smelling like a box of sterile pads. And the taste in my mouth is like that of rubber. Awful."

"Want me to go get you some ice chips?" Coop asked.

"Hey, that would be swell."

Libby sat in the chair beside Carla's bed as he left the area in search of some ice. On the way, he stopped in to visit with the moaning woman. Poor thing had her teeth removed so her mouth was a wrinkled gaping hole.

"How are things, Grandma?"

"Jimmy?" she called out.

"No, I'm Calvin. But that's okay. Can I get you anything?"

"Tell them I need more pain meds. It hurts all over. Everything hurts," her wild eyes devoured the sight of him.

She was also scared. This was the room where lots of people were scared, unlike some place like the maternity ward or a nursery.

"Are you allowed to eat?"

The woman didn't understand what he was saying, so he gave her a salute, squeezed her bony liver-spotted hand, and added, "I'll tell them. You stay right here, okay?"

"Okay, Jimmy."

Miraculously, as he walked toward the nurse's station, the woman had stopped complaining. The peace and quiet was delicious.

"Your lady there in bed eight says she needs more pain meds. But I think some cherry Jell-O would do the trick too."

"Yeah," the nurse answered him. "She's had all she can, but I'll see what we've got. Might take her mind off things. Thanks."

"No problem. Not trying to get in the way. But can you tell me where I can find some ice chips for Mrs. Brownlee, if she's allowed?"

"We've got an ice machine in the employee lounge through those doors. Paper cups and spoons are all right there too. She's already asking for food, so don't encourage the Jell-O with her just yet."

"Not a problem."

Coop brought a cup of water for Libby, another filled to the brim with ice chips, along with a spoon, and a third cup for himself. "Here you go, ma'am. Chef's special."

"Oh, that's great." She tried to sit up straighter but found she couldn't. And then as she struggled, she began to feel pain. Libby helped serve her chips with the spoon.

"That's divine. Makes you grateful for the little things in life. Oh, that's so much better."

"Can I sit here?" Coop asked, pointing to the corner of the bed.

"Of course." Sucking on a piece of ice, she closed her eyes before speaking again. "So did Dr. Green talk to you guys?"

"He did, Mom. He said you were and are a trooper."

"So where do I stand, then? He didn't tell me diddly. Not for my lack of trying, however."

Libby gave her another spoonful of chips and continued. "He said they are waiting to hear from the lab. He sent specimens into the lab—"

Coop interrupted. "They always do that, to make sure they have clear margins, meaning they got all the nasty stuff. But he did say he thought they did."

"Oh, that's good," Carla answered. She fiddled with the bandage under her right arm. "Looks like they took some nodes too. He told me in the office they might do that if they needed to. Did he talk about that?"

"Yes, Mom. He said you had a little more of the cancer than they expected."

Coop didn't think that comment would fly, so he wasn't surprised when Carla nearly bit her head off.

"Oh, come on, Libby. There's no such thing as a little cancer. If they take the lymph nodes, that means it's spread. I'm no dummy."

"I don't think you're a dummy, Mom. They're doing what will give you the result we all want. Being cautious."

Cooper nodded, studied Libby carefully, and decided to make the communication she didn't want to. "Carla, Dr. Green called Austin, so he knows."

"He did what?" She was lit up and extremely agitated.

"I'm sorry, Mom. He did it on his own direction. I told him. Well, you told him too. But he just decided to overrule that and called Dad. He's going to take a flight out tomorrow morning."

"I knew that would happen. Oh, that's too bad. Austin had been so looking forward to that event. Dammit. He's been working on that speech for over a month."

"He wants to talk to you when you feel up to it, Mom. Dr. Green told us to give you that message."

"I'll do that. I want to hear from the lab first. Did they say how long before we had results?"

"If not before dinner, then tomorrow morning, Carla. I think it depends on how busy they are," Coop answered.

"So what else did he say?"

Libby looked up at him, which was a mistake. Mrs. Brownlee rather sharply barked at her. "So what's the *bad* news? I don't like being left out of the loop."

Coop decided he'd been given the reins. "He's done everything he can. They're going to continue to run tests, probably do a scan. Again, Carla, a lot of this is routine. They want to be sure they got it all. But you're right, the lymph nodes being invaded isn't the best news in the world. But once they know the results, then they'll make up a strategy for combating this evil thing."

"And what else?"

"That was pretty much all he said," Libby whispered.

She searched Libby's face, then stared at Coop, then back to Libby again. "I'm not a child. I'm not fragile or senile. Please do me the favor of telling me the truth."

"He said to be prepared for some tough days ahead. He warned us that you needed all the strength you can muster, Carla. So he asked us to wait for the lab report before making any assumptions. We were instructed not to scare you. Beyond that, we don't know."

"Finally. Okay then. We wait. How long will I be here, did he say?"

Coop knew that with the possibility of another surgery, she wouldn't be going home right away. "It depends on what shows up on the CAT scan."

"When is that going to be?" she asked.

"Sounded like maybe tonight," said Libby. "Should I call Neil and Marsha? And can I talk to Dad, or do you want to first?"

"I want to get the results first before I call anyone."

AN HOUR LATER, Carla was wheeled into the computer imaging room and given her scan. Coop could see the site of the surgeries in the crack of the large door before they closed it. Her scars were nearly eight inches long, cut diagonally, but leaving a small skin flap that hung oddly at the edge of her upper torso for the reconstruction, should that be done.

A private hospital room was found for her, so she was returned upstairs from the imaging department to a new room with a nice view of flowering treetops. This time, the wait wasn't as long.

Dr. Green sauntered through the doorway, but he wasn't smiling.

"Oh, God. Here it comes," Carla whined.

"How are you feeling?" Dr. Green asked.

"Why don't you tell me? How *am* I doing?"

"It isn't exactly how we'd hoped. There are a couple areas where the lab said we didn't have a clear margin, and the CAT scan confirmed it. So we'll be prepping you for surgery again tomorrow morning, although this time it won't be as extensive. I have to go in a little deeper, all the way to the ribs on your right. And I'll have to take some nodes in your groin area too that showed up on the scan."

"But you're not taking anything else?"

"You mean like your uterus, female parts? Nope. Those aren't affected. We want to stop the spread, and it appears it started to a little bit. We're going to try one more time, and then you'll be on a regimen with your oncologist, who's excellent, by the way."

"Yes, I was told he was the best."

"You have as good a chance as anybody to fully recover, but don't chicken out on me. It's going to be a bit unpleasant because of how aggressive the cancer is. We have ways of matching the type and qualities of the cancer with treatments we know work very well against them. But I'm not going to lie, and I told Austin this as well. You're in for a rough patch before you'll start to feel better."

Carla's eyes were wide as fear showed up for the first time in her face. Coop could see that her dreams of being able to beat the cancer with juicing and vegetable gardening were fading by the minute.

He knew it was a good thing Austin Brownlee was coming sooner rather than later, because Carla was going to need his strength.

Dr. Death was knocking on her door, and he was an unwelcome visitor. But Coop saw in her eyes not only the fear but the determination not to give up.

He made a vow to himself that he'd never ever complain about her stubbornness again.

CHAPTER 6

LIBBY WANTED TO drop by her parents' house now that she knew her mother was going to be in the hospital and that her father would be arriving back in San Diego tomorrow sometime.

Their long-term housekeeper and sometimes cook, Ynez, was always reliable when it came to completing tasks Carla had given her, but Libby wanted to see if there were any other little items that needed attending before either her mother or her father came home. She wanted to make sure the sheets were changed and everything was warm and inviting.

She was riding in Coop's Hummer, high above the rest of the world, it seemed.

"You know, I wasn't quite sure what to expect, but your mom looked pretty good for having been beaten up today," Coop whispered.

He always did that when he wasn't sure what to say and needed to fill the space between them.

Challenge accepted.

"Today went by so fast. Before we know it, the kids will be out of the house, married, and gone. Just gone. I was struck by how quickly life comes and goes. It's so fragile. My mom was always that larger-than-life figure in my world, a leader, inspirational. It was a shock to see her so small and wiped out. She was trying really hard to be tough. But all I could see was what a tender, fragile thread we all cling to."

He quickly glanced over at her and then positioned his eyes back on the road. "She wants to live, Libby. I could see that loud and clear."

"She does, doesn't she?" That was the fear Libby saw in her face—like life would be taken from her before she could complete her work. "She doesn't like to leave things halfway. She'll be very busy, tidying up loose ends and crossing things off her list. There will be no stopping her."

"In a way," he began tenderly, "she has a hard deadline. Or the scare of one."

"Exactly. God called on her today and asked if she was ready. And she didn't like the question."

"Believe me, I can see that conversation." He chuckled. "She's going to need a job some day when she makes it to Heaven. Either that, or she'll start disrupting things so she has to go in and re-organize them."

Libby felt a chill when she realized they were talking about her mother's death, not her mother's recovery.

"You better give your brother and father a call when we get there."

"I intend to. In a way, I'm glad Dr. Green called him. Now that we know what's beginning to be presented to us, it would have been a mistake to have my father come home from Japan and then find out about my mother's surgery. He wouldn't want that decision taken away from him."

"He's going to be devastated."

"He is. He discusses nearly everything with her, and now he's going to feel lost. Even when she's sick, he can't function. He doesn't know how to make coffee in their expensive espresso maker, and she does all the meal planning and cooking, with help from Ynez. If she goes away, she prepares meals for him to warm up. He'll take it harder than Mom will—or, at least, harder than she'll let on she does."

"Maybe he'll surprise you."

Coop's comment was a nice attempt at lightening up the subject matter. "I hope they both do. It's going to take the two of them working on this thing together. But you're right. They are an unbreakable partnership, and that's what's made their marriage so strong. That's really good news, Coop. For some people, when tragedy strikes, they run to their separate corners. That won't be their way."

"Yup. Well, let's hope God punched her library card and got her an extension."

"I'm hoping the same thing."

THE SPANISH-STYLE HOME was colorful this time of year. The light conch hue on the stucco exterior with dark wrought iron trim and custom-made window latches and door handles was the backdrop to a bright display of summer flowers, and although it was still early in the season, the plants Carla had grown along the sides of the walkway were bursting with color. Her mother loved her flower gardens, both her one in front and the larger cut flower garden in the back by the patio.

Libby was relieved to see that the gardeners had done a nice job making sure the place looked sparkling and inviting for the owners' homecoming.

They entered through the massive dark mahogany front door and stood in the foyer. It was where she met Coop for the very first time, when he dropped by to pay his respects to her father on orders from Kyle Lansdown. It was a custom Kyle adhered to, trying to soothe the pain of losing his whole family by visiting the family of a fallen SEAL, who had also been a medic for his team, like Cooper.

Same as today, she hadn't been ready for this new intruder entering their home, bringing up a story about Dr. Brownlee's twin brother's death. She smiled as she thought how much attitude she'd given him that day. But after he left, she couldn't get him out of her mind.

She searched the ceiling in the grand entrance, which always made her feel like she was entering a small church.

Coop came up behind her and placed his palm at the top of her spine, rubbing her shoulders and neck, as if he knew she was thinking about that first day they'd met. The truth was, she remembered that meeting every single time she entered this room.

Ynez had cut flowers and placed them in a large pitcher on the living room coffee table, just like her mother did nearly every day. It was the first thing her dad noticed each time he came home and commented on frequently.

As a child, Libby used to hide behind those flowers if they had a guest she didn't want to talk to, since the sprays of color completely dominated her tiny frame.

She walked to the grand staircase and jogged up the steps to check on the guest rooms and their master. Everything was as it should be. Ynez even put another large bouquet on the highboy dresser in their master and a smaller one in the master bath between the two matching his and hers sinks. Her mother's toothbrush was setting beside the sink on the right. Her father's was missing but usually along the sink to the left.

She pulled the bedspread tight and smoothed over the pillows, straightening one that had been placed crooked. She double-checked that their towels had been freshly washed too, and they had.

With another few minutes of checking the other rooms and baths, her work was done. Everything was in perfect condition. She began walking down the stairway where Cooper had poured himself a glass of water and was staring out at the pool and patio grounds outside.

From the backside, Coop and her dad had the same build, both exceedingly tall—her father was only an inch or so shorter than her husband. They both had no hips, a slim waist, flat butt, and very long legs. Often people thought he was their biological son and Libby married into the family.

Cooper turned and greeted her with a warm smile. "Everything okay? You want me to help you with anything?"

"No, Ynez did a wonderful job. I didn't expect otherwise, but she filled the house with flowers, more than usual, and Mom'll like that. So will my dad."

They hugged. She watched the ripples on the turquoise pool water from a slight breeze that had picked up in the afternoon. The lawn outside of the patio was freshly cut. The hoses were wrapped in circles, all done in the same direction, as her father liked. Everything was waiting on the two of them to come home. The stage was set.

"Sure have had some wonderful parties here over the years, haven't we?"

"Your parents have always been very generous. They've hosted receptions here, adopted Team Guys who came from scattered families. Your mom could make them feel comfortable, loved. They make it look easy, don't they?"

"They do. Kinda like we do. We train over and over again, so the muscle memory kicks in when we're faced with an unexpected situation. And—"

Libby finished the sentence with him, because they were always the same words.

"Everything is always unexpected," they said together.

"You Team guys make it look easy too. It's almost like this house has a procedure, a way they do things. I was just noticing the hoses, the arrangement of the patio furniture, with clean seating pads. Ynez always washes down the glass-top table when she sweeps the patio."

Coop squeezed her closer to him, looking down on her. "And always after the leaf blowers are used by the gardener, not before."

"Of course not." She rested her head against him. "I didn't mind the structure because each time I opened a drawer here in the kitchen, I saw the same things arranged the same way every time. There was never a Plan A and Plan B to this house. There's only one way, and it's been that way for nearly twenty years now."

"Now, that's different than the Teams. We prepare for Plan A, Plan B, Plan C, and on down the line until Kyle and the high-ups are satisfied we've taken everything into account, and even then—"

Libby again helped him complete the words. "No mission ever goes as planned," they said together. Coop continued, "Something always goes wrong."

"Maybe that's what she fears most," Libby sighed.

"Could be. You mean, her schedule is going to change. She's going to go to work to create a new routine to conquer this disease. And it won't be juicing or raising fresh vegetables and taking vitamins. I think she's got that idea now."

"Beginning to. She's going to have to learn to be flexible and patient. She'll be like those young kids who waltz in here and haven't had anyone cook for them in years, who excel at flower arranging and throwing perfect parties where even the barbeque is cooked to perfection."

She giggled at her own words.

"The person who usually takes care of others has to learn how to be taken care of," Coop said perceptively.

"Exactly."

"You want some water?" he asked, moving toward the sink to refill his.

"Yes, please."

While Coop added ice and water to a tall glass, Libby sat in the small family room off the kitchen and dialed her dad's cell.

"Hi. How was Japan this time, Dad?"

"From what I could see of it, busy. I recorded my speech a few minutes ago on my cell and sent it off to the committee.

For the first time in my life, it will be a virtual keynote address that will air while I'm on an airplane."

"That's a creative solution."

"Necessity is the mother of all inventions, Libby. We improvise."

"So what time do you get in?"

"It will be late. I think it's ten."

"Okay, so I'd like to talk to you about Mom."

"Please. Fill me in."

"First off, she'll have to have more surgery tomorrow. There are a couple troubling areas they've identified he has to go back and get."

"Not a very good sign, then," her father said. "Where is this?"

"I'm not exactly sure, but I think he said on her right, very close to her ribs, and he might have to scrape away one little area where it might have attached. And there are a couple lymph nodes in her groin area that lit up on the CAT scan. Until she's healed up, we can't start radiation treatment." It was a mouthful, but Libby wanted to give him everything without holding back.

"Ouch. That's a lot. I never heard a peep out of her, did you? Did she ever complain?"

"No, she never did. She was sleeping more, though. Remember?"

"Yes. She was supposed to come with me this trip but told me she felt she didn't have the energy. Honestly, I should have insisted she see a doctor right away."

"Good luck convincing her to do something she doesn't

want to do. Dr. Green made a point of telling her she shouldn't have waited so long. So she knows this. Not that it matters."

"You should have called me before the surgery, Libby. I was very disappointed."

"And you know that was her idea, Dad."

"All the same, you should have overruled her. What if something had happened on the operating table and I never got a chance to say good-bye? No, that was an error in judgment."

It didn't take Libby very long to feel guilty about her part in the temporary coverup. Although she considered him the closest member of her family outside of Coop and the kids, he always used the criticism of an "error in judgment" as the top of his list of most egregious mistakes. And that would be the end of it. It was always her mother who would never let her forget her error, constantly reinforcing it over and over again to avoid it happening again. But Libby had learned something her brother never did. It was faster to just acknowledge it and go on than to fight about it. Neil had been at odds so many times with their mother that the relationship was permanently scarred. And even his wife, Marsha, had frequently rocked the boat, and they hardly ever spoke. They acted civil but avoided engagement as much as possible.

Libby was going to try to bridge that gap, if she could.

"You're right, Dad. I promised her I wouldn't tell anyone. It was what she asked of me, and I thought I was helping her out. But I was wrong."

She nodded her thanks to Cooper, who had brought her the water and a sliced red apple in a bowl.

Silence on the other end of the call worried her.

"Dad, are you okay?"

"Was Dr. Green any more hopeful than he was with me? I kind of got it both barrels at once. I think he spent more time telling me what could happen than what we could do to help combat this enemy. He has a lousy bedside manner, even though we've been friends for years."

Libby mused about that one. "She said the same thing, Dad."

"Good. Well, I'm going to give Carla a call now that I've heard from you. She never called me. Did the nurse tell you about my request that she do so?"

"We all told her. Even Dr. Green told her."

"Sometimes she gets this attitude that if she doesn't talk about it, it never happened, and we can't do that with this particular illness."

"You're so right. We're kind of in the fact-finding stages of things right now. I think everyone is looking for indicators, clues to what we can expect and what the effective treatment is. I think that's the hardest part, really. The not knowing is what wears people out. But I have confidence they'll give us more information tomorrow after she has the second surgery, and although you'll be on your flight, I'll leave you a voicemail so that as soon as you land, you can be brought up to speed."

"Good. So her spirit is strong, then?"

"When has it not been, Dad? You could call it strong or stubborn. And I agree with Dr. Green. In the long run, that will help her."

"Okay, Libby. Cooper isn't still in North Carolina, is he?"

"No, he's right here with me. He came back yesterday. He sends his love and prayers."

"Oh, thank you. Well, are you going to call Neil, or should I?"

"Let me call him because I may have more details than you do. I think they're going to want to come, or at least Neil will. What should I—"

"Neil makes more money than I do. He can afford to stay at a hotel. I want to keep the guest rooms for some help we'll have to hire, perhaps nurses when she gets home. And of course, if you come over, we'd ask you to stay. But I don't think Neil and Marsha and especially the three girls should stay at the house. I think it would be too upsetting, don't you?"

"Probably. So I won't ask. And I don't have the room. So that's that."

"I'm going to sign off now. You sure she feels well enough for a short chat?"

"Make it short. She's going to go into overtime trying to convince you she feels fine. But I think she'd love to hear your voice. Just do it now. Don't wait. She's probably going to need to rest for tomorrow."

"Okay, my dear. Give my best to Dr. Green and give a hug and kiss to Cooper for me and tell him thanks. I'm glad he's able to be close."

"For now, Dad. But they are going to work up soon, so I'll be managing everything solo in a bit. They won't give him time off unless it's critical."

"Thanks for calling, Libby. I love you."

"Love you too, Dad."

Libby breathed a sigh of relief after she hung up. She hadn't realized she'd held so much tension during the call.

"Let's do some box breathing, Libby," said Cooper, sitting on the coffee table in front of her. He inhaled, blocking one nostril, held his breath, and encouraged her to do the same. Then he let the air out of his lungs by plugging up the other one and exhaling. They repeated this several rotations until Libby began to relax.

"Want another apple?" he asked.

"No, I'm fine. Let's go grab some dinner after I make this call to Neil."

"Anyplace you want, sweetheart. You're doing just fine."

"I wasn't too critical of Mom?"

"It was accurate, Libby. We're in uncharted waters here."

She dialed Neil's number and found it disconnected. So she called his old land line, and he picked up after two rings.

"Hey sis. It's been a long time. Nearly a year now, right?"

"Yes, Neil. Look, I'm afraid I have some bad news. Mom's in the hospital, and they've just removed both breasts because she's been diagnosed with breast cancer. They had to act fast because it's a very aggressive form of cancer."

"Oh, Geez. Is she going to be okay?"

"We don't quite know. We'll learn more tomorrow. After the surgery, they did more testing and a scan and found more places they have to remove, so she's having that tomorrow morning."

"Okay. So does Mom or Dad want to see me? Should I fly out there, sis?"

"It's up to you, Neil. I don't think it's urgent, but you

should try to come out sometime soon."

"I don't think they want my kind of moral support. At least that last meeting didn't end well. It's not very convenient for me. I'm kind of in between jobs right now."

"Oh, I'm sorry, Neil."

"I'm over it. The hotel wanted to bring in some new blood. I thought I'd be transferred to another property, but they let me go. I have my feelers out to several other outfits. But you know how it is. At least Marsha is working."

"Well, if it comes to that and you need help with the plane reservations, Coop and I could help out." She looked up at her husband who was frowning. "I mean, we could help bring you out. We can't send all five of you. You understand."

Cooper nodded and placed a smile on his face. Then he gave her a thumbs-up.

"Well, that's nice, sis. So let me talk it over with Marsha. You'll call me tomorrow after the surgery and let me know how it went?"

"Absolutely."

"Well, I gotta go. Um, we're supposed to be somewhere, and everyone's ready."

It was late back in Colorado so she wondered where he would be going. The sun was beginning to set in California.

They said their good-byes, and they both hung up.

Libby splashed water on her face to shake her mood and tried to hit the reset button. Her eyes were dry, and she imagined they looked red. She considered telling Coop they could skip dinner, but at that moment, the front doorbell chimed.

Cooper took several long strides and opened the door. Standing before him was a blonde woman, tall but not willowy. She wore stretch long running pants that showed her enormous bulging thigh muscles. Her bright orange Nike's had yellow laces. Her tanned face contrasted well with her piercing blue eyes, just like Cooper's. Her hair was wiry and a slightly lighter shade than his. She wore several string bracelets and a black silicone band. Around her neck, she wore a choker made with shells.

"Can I help you?" Cooper asked.

"Are you a Brownlee by any chance?" she asked. Her wide smile revealed large white teeth polished smooth. Her lips were smeared with a rose-colored lip gloss.

"No. But my wife is." He turned to Libby, placing his palm at the back of her waist.

"I'm Libby Brownlee."

The young woman held out her hand. "Nice to meet you. I'm Karen Watson. I think I am your cousin. Probably a cousin you never thought you had!"

Libby was trying to do some calculations in her head. She appeared to be similar age to both she and Cooper, but she couldn't do the math on exactly how she could be related.

"Are you sure you have the right Brownlee family?"

"Oh, I'm quite sure. Your father's name is Austin Brownlee. He's a doctor, right?"

"Yes, he is." Libby wasn't sure she wanted to let the young woman inside, so they continued their conversation from the doorway.

"And he had a twin brother named Will Brownlee, right?"

"Right." Now Coop began to wrap his hand around her waist and slowly pulled her towards him.

"I'm Will's daughter. I was born after he died."

"But—where did you—"

"My mother never told me about you guys. I grew up north. Anyway, I'd always wanted to know about my dad, so I had some DNA testing done, and it turns out your father's DNA is on file, and there's a nearly exact match. At first, I thought your dad was my father, but that's a whole other story."

"You've talked to my dad?"

"No. I haven't. Is he home? I would like to meet him."

"He's on a business trip," Cooper said tersely. "Maybe we could take your information, and we could have him call you when he gets back?"

"Oh, that would be cool. I'm down here to participate in the Coronado Marathon in two weeks. Came down to train, so I thought I'd look you guys up." She got a notepad out from her black pants zipper pocket. She quickly wrote a number down and handed Cooper the piece of paper. He took it like it was diseased.

"Thanks," he said. "I'll have him call you when he gets a chance."

"So, just so I can explain this to my dad, your mother never told you who your father was?"

"Nope. Just said he was dead. It wasn't a serious relationship, she said. Not like they were engaged or anything. They dated a few times, and he left for his job and never came back. She found out he was killed the same day she found out she was pregnant and so decided to move back up north. That's where I was born."

Libby was trying to figure out if she believed this stranger. Coop stepped in and made the decision for her.

"It was nice meeting you, Karen, but I'm afraid we're on our way to run a couple of errands. We'll encourage Libby's dad to give you a call after he settles back in. We'll leave that up to him, okay?"

She shrugged. "Sure. Whatever." She smiled and stepped toward Libby, but Coop blocked her. "Oops."

"I'm sorry."

"Are you a cop? You act like a cop."

"No."

She squinted her right eye and angled her head to the side. "Would you mind if I gave a good-bye hug to my cuz here? She's the first person outside of my mom who I'm actually related to."

Cooper reluctantly stepped back and within a couple of seconds, Karen's long arms were wrapped around Libby. She moved from side to side as if they were going to dance. Then she just as quickly pulled her arms back and straightened up, addressing Cooper, leaving Libby frozen in place.

"So I guess you're my cuz as well. Nice to meet you!" She suddenly wrapped her arms around Cooper and gave him a kiss on his cheek.

Libby wanted to peel her arms away from her husband, send her back from where she came from, and hope she never returned. If she got her hands on that note, she intended to tear it up. Coop had put it in his back pocket.

A good washing would take care of that problem.

They watched as she jumped into a dented older orange Toyota with a spare tire without a hubcap on the passenger side rear and drove away, leaving a trail of smoke behind. Before she rounded the corner, she honked and waved out of the sunroof.

Cooper took in a deep breath.

"One thing I already know about her," he said.

"What's that?" Libby asked as she slipped her fingers through his.

"Her timing is horrible."

CHAPTER 7

COOP FELT A little ashamed about how he'd treated the new Brownlee cousin—if she was indeed Libby's cousin. But it was an issue of protecting his wife's family, since the relationship hadn't been verified. He also felt it was a little forward to just come knocking on the Brownlee home without calling first. So he decided he'd been the proper amount of frosty under the circumstances.

He put the guilt out of his mind and concentrated on driving Libby and himself to their favorite Italian restaurant.

Libby called Gillian and Will at Luci and Danny Begay's house, making sure they'd been picked up and were going to do their homework. Will liked playing with their three boys who were all very close in age. Gillian was tough enough to hang with the boys as well and, although she wasn't a teenager yet, managed to successfully create an environment where they fought over her attention.

Cooper thought about the tour they'd done in Iraq several years ago when Danny had befriended the young Iraqi boy, who he would later adopt, and his father, who was trying to smuggle the two of them out of the country to safety. They had lived a nomadic life in burned out and bombed buildings scrounging for food after the death of the rest of their family. And although the little boy's father was in the conscripted militia, he hadn't shown up for work recently and stayed with the boy twenty-four seven, a violation that was punishable by public execution.

Dozens of their friends had left the country already or had been killed.

Danny and young Ali had formed a friendship because Ali spent all day throwing rocks with deadly accuracy. It was sometimes the source of their meal at night, their one meal a day, if he could kill a pigeon or escaped chicken. They'd even eaten black birds, Danny told them one night. The father and son were holed up in an abandoned soccer stadium, hiding from bands of militia and bandits. Once discovered, the SEALs shared what food they could spare with the two of them while they awaited permission and information on the extraction.

So Danny fashioned a slingshot from some bits of catheter tubing and a piece of rubber from an innertube. The hardest part of making the weapon was finding a stick of the right size with the strength to handle the tension as the rubber catheter material was pulled back to expel a projectile. Ali kept the slingshot with him all day and slept with it at night. He also kept a small pocket of smooth stones, all about the same size, just in case they needed something or to ward off someone who was going to take advantage of them.

And it turned out to be what saved young Ali's life. A roving criminal band of youths and adult males discovered they were living in an abandoned soccer stadium and captured Ali's father, threatening to harm him if he didn't come back. The SEALs had gotten permission to evacuate the two of them, so a big bird had just landed for the pickup. Everyone was on board, and Danny encouraged Ali not to turn around, to keep running for his arms. One of the gang members quickly gained on the boy and was going to overtake him.

At the worst possible moment, Ali tripped and fell to his knees. He quickly recovered, rolling onto his back just in time to take out his slingshot and drill a fairly large pebble at the oncoming man, hitting him right in the forehead with such force they could all hear the crack of his skull.

His father tried to defend himself against impossible odds and would be tortured and perhaps killed after many days of abuse if not rescued. And there was no way a rescue was possible any longer. They'd all seen it happen too many times to the wives, sons, and daughters of their interpreters and others who helped the American forces and their hopeless mission of peace.

Coop would never forget that scene, little Ali running into Danny's arms, running for his life, for his freedom, and leaving everything else about his past behind. One of the snipers put the father out of his misery but not before he got to see that his son had made it to safety.

Ali was so strong for his age that, when they enrolled him in Kindergarten a year later, he was clever enough, strong enough, and fast enough to outmaneuver kids double his size and age. Will loved spending time with this now nine-year-old boy who, in many ways, was more a man than most of the fathers in their school. He was fearless and never without his slingshot.

Coop suspected that the two of them would be getting into some trouble together as they grew into teens and beyond. Many of the SEAL kids often did.

Libby put the phone back in her purse and sighed. "From the sounds coming from the boys' room, I think the idea of completing homework is a bridge too far." She leaned against the door of the truck, resting her elbow on the windowsill and palming her forehead.

"Let them burn off some steam. They can get serious tomorrow," said Coop.

"I think you're right. Boy, I don't know how Luci does it, surrounded by men."

"Hey, we're not all bad. We have our talents."

"Honey, I'm not talking about you, of course. She threatened Danny she'd take one of the boys to their church Mother-Daughter luncheon if he didn't 'borrow' a daughter from someone else. She's going to talk to Gillian tonight about it."

"She'd probably like that."

They drove in silence the rest of the way.

At their table, the waiter started to pour Cooper some wine, and he refused it. He took Libby's hand while they waited for their salads. "What do you really think about Karen?"

"I don't know. It's going to be a shock to Dad. Did she say where her mother was?"

"Nope."

"What a day." Libby shook her head. "Could it get any

stranger?"

"Mrs. Cooper, why don't we just enjoy the candlelight, the wonderful food, and then have a nice relaxing evening at home? We could turn in early."

"That sounds divine. Perhaps a little hot tub party is on the agenda."

"Anything you want, sweetheart."

They made it through dinner and the drive home. They sat together in the warm hot tub and observed the stars since it was so clear. Libby's cell phone lay right next to Cooper's on the folded towels while they listened to the distant waves. Cooper reached for her, and she melted into him with a long languid kiss leading to so much more.

One of the phones rang.

Libby put her forehead against Coop's. "I don't believe this."

"Who's going to look?" he asked her, knowing he'd be the one to dry off and answer the phone. Their workup was too close. These were the days when he couldn't be out of contact for more than a few minutes. They'd all gotten the warning straight from Kyle.

He watched her lovely face, her nose and forehead wrinkled in a frown, her eyes shut tight, willing the rest of the world to go away. He stood up, climbed out of the tub, and grabbed his phone with his towel. In the night air, dripping wet, he heard the voice of his LPO on the other line.

"Coop, we leave in the morning. Oh eight hundred."

"This is confirmed."

"If you think you'll oversleep, come on down now. Several

of the guys are bunking here tonight."

"Sir?"

"No, I'm at home with Christy."

Cooper saw Libby's sad face in the moonlight. Reaching over to touch her cheek, he continued with his conversation. "Can you tell me where?"

"Mexico. Cabo again. Just like before. Shorts and flamingo or flowered shirts. Bring a hat. You need to do a little rescue mission on that pelt of yours. Your brains are beginning to show."

He would have laughed, because it was funny, but he wasn't in the mood.

"How long?" He leaned over the hot tub again and kissed his wife.

"Short one. We got a target. We might go back later and do more, but that's why the urgency. They've kidnapped some volunteers working the border. All girls again. Sorority sisters from a Catholic girls college doing their civic duty."

"God dammit."

"We have to save them. That's what we do, Coop."

"Yes, that's what we do."

THE BEST THING about going to Mexico was that he didn't have to pack much, and taking arms over the border was prohibited, so they had to liaison with their State Department rep, who had already worked out the permissions. It wasn't like Africa, where sometimes permissions were impossible because no one was sure who was really in charge to ask permission.

But that was the protocol, hammered out and paid for in

advance through foreign aid monies.

So he was feeling the steam smoking off his body still as he shoved his things into the black duffel bag with the black Trident logo stitched in and barely visible. It only took him about ten minutes, because his medic pack was always restocked after the last deployment so he could grab it and be ready in an emergency. And he didn't have to bring enough extra supplies to help run a clinic out in the middle of the jungle where supplies were auctioned off like gold.

He lingered at the doorway a few seconds. Libby was fast asleep in their bed.

He'd been looking forward to a night of lovemaking, this time not for Libby's sake but his own. The family dynamics were changing. A lot had changed in just one day. He wanted to keep it strong and tight. That's what he told himself, anyhow, as he slipped into the bed next to her soft skin.

He was quiet as he wrapped his arms around her, buried his nose in the back of her neck, and found a comfortable part of the pillow to lay his head against.

And then a miracle happened.

Libby turned in his arms and kissed him. "I need you," she whispered into his lips.

"Thank God!"

CHAPTER 8

LIBBY LEFT FOR the hospital the same time Cooper left for base. That meant she was nearly an hour early.

Sneaking down the hallway of the surgery ward, where shifts were changing and before any of the meal service people and cleaning personnel showed up, she was practically invisible. Her mother's private room door was shut, probably to aid in her sleep. Libby knew how noisy hospitals could be and how nearly impossible it was to get a decent rest.

But her mother was snoring up a storm because she was forced to sleep on her back due to the bandages. And she was completely wiped out in what Libby thought was probably a drug-induced near-coma. Without waking her, she positioned herself on the chair beside her mother's bed and waited.

Cooper had told her he was feeling a little guilty for his behavior with Karen yesterday. Libby disagreed, telling him he didn't owe the stranger any courtesy. Part of that was that this type of news wasn't something her mother needed right now. And if there was a woman her mother's age out there who had dated a man who looked identical to her dad, Libby could understand why her mom wouldn't exactly be welcoming. She just couldn't take the risk. She didn't want to encourage Karen or anyone to intervene.

Coop was right. Her timing was terrible.

At last, a prep crew came in, surprised that she'd been allowed to stay there. She was ushered out before her mother woke up with instructions to make sure to let Carla know she was waiting downstairs. She quickly picked up some scrambled eggs at the cafeteria and a cup of strong black coffee. This time, Dr. Green didn't come looking for her, since they all knew what was going to be done. It was the outcome she was most interested in.

She called Luci Begay to get an update on the kids and was reassured everyone got off to school on time.

"But Danny had to lower the boom last night. He threatened corporal punishment, and you should have seen Will's eyes."

"Yeah, Coop has a rather gentle approach to discipline. But with your brood, I certainly can understand it."

"They used to gang up on Griffin, remember?"

Griffin was their youngest, and for weeks after Ali came to live with them, the child's greatest occupational hazard was getting nailed with a packet of jam when his parents weren't looking, since Ali and the slingshot were inseparable. It frequently had to be handed over to Danny.

"I do remember that."

"They're thick as thieves now. It just took Griffin a few years to catch up. So now they go after Chester. He's the one with jam and catsup direct hits plastered all over his face and neck."

"I've told you several times, Luci. You're a saint."

"I had a nice long discussion with Gillian. She'll probably ask you if she can go to the luncheon with me. I could use a little girl time. She seemed to relate to that."

Libby chuckled and promised to encourage it.

"You know, Libby, she's a real beauty. Coop and Will are going to have their hands full when she gets into high school. I don't envy your job."

"Well, we take it a day at a time, don't we?"

"We sure do. How's your mom doing? Did the surgery go well?"

"That's what I was calling you about today. I should be able to pick the kids up after school, but if I get in a jam, can I ask you to keep them one more day?"

"No problem. But what's the situation?"

"She's gone in for more surgery this morning, because apparently, they didn't get it all."

"Oh, poor thing. Bless her heart. Do you want me to bring the kids by to see her, or can she have visitors?"

"She can't, Luci. Especially the kids right now. I'm waiting for confirmation that she can come home today or tomorrow."

"Not on the day of surgery. It will be tomorrow at the earliest. But let her stay as long as she wants to rest. She's going to need it."

"Good point."

Libby agreed to touch base with her later on in the morning as they said their good-byes.

She remained in the waiting area, like the morning before, and checked out the screen showing the flow of patients. Her mom was still in surgery.

About an hour later, Dr. Green showed up dressed in his scrubs, his facemask hanging from one ear. He motioned for her to join him in the hallway again.

"She tolerated everything really well. She's a great patient because she's so strong. But I had a little bit of trouble with the lymph nodes at her groin area. It's a delicate procedure, and I didn't want to mess up something, causing some incontinence. She'll be on a cancer treatment that will be laced with hormones when she gets into that routine, so I don't think we should be too concerned about it if we didn't get everything. What's left is probably microscopically small. But you need to understand it's very likely it will show up somewhere else."

"Are those aggressive cancers hard to monitor? Hard to stop?"

"Oh God no. In many ways, they are the most dangerous but the most treatable. Unless you don't get it all. But since she's already going to be seen for chemo and perhaps some radiation—"

"You didn't say anything about radiation yesterday, Doctor."

"We weren't sure at first. But I think it's a good idea. My partner will go over all that when you meet him next week."

"Are you going to do more testing then today to see if she can come home?"

"We always test the tissue samples. That's routine. But as far as another scan, she's been through a lot. Even if there was some tiny piece still left, I don't want to open her up a third time. But I didn't see anything abnormal or discolored or involving any of the major organs. That means she'll have a more enjoyable recovery period."

"That's good news. So when can she go home?"

"I want to keep her overnight, monitor her pain meds, and then perhaps tomorrow. Austin gets in today, right?"

"Late tonight, yes."

"I'm sure she'll like having him help with the transition." Dr. Green's eyes were kind and very observant. She could see he was hesitant to say something, but he eventually changed his mind and started, "I'm a bit concerned about you, Libby. Are you sleeping? Probably the best thing you can do is to go home and rest. This is a big burden on the families."

"As it goes, Coop was deployed this morning, so I think I'll take your advice and go home and crash. My girlfriend has agreed to keep the kids another day if I need it, and I'm going to take her up on it."

"Man, the hits just keep on coming, don't they? I honestly don't see how all you wives and families survive this lifestyle."

"We're a team too."

"I guess so. I don't see how else you could do it. Well, remember your mother and your kids are going to depend on you, especially at this time, so you want to do a little catch up on that sleep. I can give you something, if you want."

"No, I don't take anything. I don't want to start."

"Well, you reach out if that changes."

Libby made a quick stop at the grocery store to pick up some milk and cereal and a couple of other things and then headed for home.

She straightened the bed she was going to crash into soon.

She picked up Coop's flannel pajama bottoms he'd left on the floor and tossed them into the hamper. She straightened the towel he used, first pulling it up to her nose where she could still smell the remnants of soap and aftershave.

Shedding her clothes, she carefully slipped into bed. The cool cotton sheets were delicious. Just before she dozed off, Coop sent a text message filled with hearts and kisses, letting her know that they landed in Cabo and that they hoped to only be gone a week, two at the most.

It made her smile. She texted him back, "I'm naked in bed. I can't wait until you're home again!" She used her emoji figure to blow kisses at him.

He answered with his emoji and the caption, "Hold that thought!"

CHAPTER 9

THE STATE DEPARTMENT procured an older, vacant hotel targeted for demolition, out of the main downtown area and far enough from the marina, party boats, and bars. Kyle invited Cooper to room with him, since there was one master suite he was assigned.

They had only elected to take the ten members who went on the last deployment, considered a temporary deployment or TDI because of the quick turnaround and expected time spent. One exception to that was the substitution of Jameson Daniels for Danny Begay. Jameson was due to re-up, and if he did so while on deployment, he was owed a bonus he wouldn't get otherwise in the states.

Jameson and Lizzie had their third daughter a month ago, and with the bills piling up, he needed this bonus. Danny had some work he needed to do for the tribe, helping them write a grant proposal for new equipment the schools needed on the Navajo Reservation, where Luci grew up and Danny escaped from. But, with Luci watching Coop and Libby's two, he decided to work from home, instead of traveling to Arizona. This allowed him to stay home and help her out. Besides,

Jameson was one of Danny's best friends on the team, and he wanted the former Nashville star to get what he was fully owed by Uncle Sam. He'd earned it.

Cooper was unpacking his things to get rid of some pretty serious wrinkles.

"Can I ask you, Kyle, why we didn't bring Sven and Kelly?"

"They aren't available. Kelly was tapped to testify at a Human Rights Council at the World Health Organization. It's a week-long conference. With her experience, our president didn't give her a choice. The U.N. Ambassador is accompanying her, and Sven insisted on going as well."

"Good for her. About time we get some international cooperation," Coop answered.

"Lip service, anyway. Let's hope for more. But yes, I think it's a good sign. You'll get a kick out of this one. Some of the member nations on the panel discussions are the same ones who make tons of money off the human trafficking or allow the payoffs to change their minds on enforcement. Ambassador Gordon wants Kelly to tell him who the good guys are and who are the bad buys. Can you believe that?"

"No shit. Kind of a scary thought."

"We've been saying this ever since I joined my first platoon. Identifying who the enemy is can sometimes be the hardest part. Remember that mission on the Canaries? The former Secretary of State met up with his boyhood friend, someone he grew up playing soccer and went to Stanford with, and they still killed the poor man."

"I remember. Porter Harrison. That was a real tough one."

"Well, it exposed our vulnerability and the fact that our

intel was faulty. So Kelly, and Sven as well, will help the Ambassador out."

"At least they can stop the millions of dollars of foreign aid request getting passed by those guys."

"Yeah, Kelly's great. She's tapped all the time to give briefings to senior members of the administration. We gotta stop her from going into business with her former father-in-law for that secret private commando unit. She'll take Sven and half a dozen SEALs and beat cops with her."

"All our best, most knowledgeable people," Coop remarked, sitting on his single bed. Kyle quickly observed this.

"No, you don't, Coop. You take the queen. I'm not going to be responsible for you falling out of bed and getting injured. I can make do with this one, no problem."

"Nah, I'm okay."

"Would you quit-the-fuck-up and let me do a favor for you?"

"I'm trying to show respect," Coop argued.

"It's not disrespectful to let you have the bigger bed. You've earned it."

Coop was concerned something was going on with Kyle. He was wound up tight and arguing with everyone. That wasn't like him.

"I'm not asking for any special favors, Kyle. Seriously, you're the boss. I'm just the medic. So tell me, what's got you riled?"

Kyle sat at the edge of the queen bed, his shoulders drooping. "We're pregnant again."

Coop nearly split a gut.

"You're worried about that? You are having sex with your wife, right?"

"Yes, it's mine. No worries there."

"Oh good, cause for a minute, I thought you were pulling a Fredo on me."

"No, no. That's not it."

"Well then what, you studly Bone Frog? When you say 'we' you don't mean to say you've got one growing in *your* belly now, right?"

"Fuck no!"

"Well, my man. Just dwell in it. You are some rocket-firing love-obsessed baby-maker. That's what you are! Embrace the cactus, Kyle."

That got Kyle smiling. Then he started an impossible-to-stop snickering fit and finally broke out in waves of laughter, shaking his head. "Where do you get this shit, Coop? I know for a fact Libby doesn't talk like that."

Coops stood up and pretended to be annoyed with him, just to needle him further. "As a matter of fact, hell no she doesn't talk to me like that. She talks to me in nice, loving words that make me get all nasty because she's so sweet. Man, if she wanted to, I'd have ten kids. I'd retire and buy a farm just to keep them all working. No shit!"

Kyle knew he'd been played with, and it didn't bother him one bit. "Now I get what you're saying. You're saying I need to be grateful for what I've got. And I am. I love all the things I can do with my dick that has to do with Christy."

Behind Cooper, he heard a small crowd whisper, "Woo." He turned and saw four Team Guys hovering in the doorway to their bedroom.

"Hey!" He lunged for them and they all disappeared. Kyle was still chuckling, focusing on the tiled floor.

Coop jabbed him one more time, gently. "You're gonna love this child. You're gonna love watching her grow, getting big. You're gonna not worry about the interruption to her business, because you'll see, Christy will probably have a record year. You're gonna be grateful you're married to a woman who outearns you by three times."

Kyle listened with a smirk on his face. That told Coop he was hitting the mark.

Cooper leaned forward and whispered, "But at night, with all the kids in their beds and the lights out, you're the master. You love the hell out of that woman because she wants every piece of you she can have, and you'll love every minute giving it to her. You're the king of the castle, the most important and miraculous man in her whole world. And she's gonna make you buy more diapers, and I'm guessing you've got to get more baby furniture again. You won't worry about all the cost because she's making a shit-pile of money, but you'd love her even if you were as poor as could be. You've been blessed, Kyle. And I feel lucky, too, to be able to serve with you and be mentored on how to be a good man because, Kyle Fuckin' Lansdowne, *you are that man!*"

He could see Kyle was conflicted as to how he should respond.

"Is this for reals, Coop?"

"Yessir, it is. Like I said, embrace the cactus, and maybe next year, you can do a Ted Talk."

COOPER WAS QUESTIONED about his little speech by several on the team. Jameson was the first to speak up.

"I feel like I'm in that musical. *What did I miss?*"

"You know we go way back. He was getting a bit heavy thinking about something, and I made fun of him. But that's all I'm going to say."

By the time he'd uttered that, Jason and Damon were standing next to him.

"Hey, Coop, does this have anything to do with the mission?" asked Damon.

Cooper stared at him as if he was wearing a donut on his head. "I was talking about making babies. How in hell did you think that had anything to do with our mission? That's the dumbest question I've ever heard, Damon. And you know it."

Damon shrugged and was a good sport about it.

"So Christy's pregnant," said Jameson. "We gotta get some Cubans to celebrate."

"I'd watch that if I were you. We wait for the announcement, and then we celebrate, just in case this isn't the exciting event of the year, okay?"

"Point well taken. But I personally think the team should help him with some names for the new one. Something like Bevis or Guido or Lance Lansdowne, something like that. I'm not going to be able to help myself, Coop."

"You do too much of that, and I'll throw your guitar out of the helicopter next time."

Jason cleared his throat, interrupting. "Something in this room is going all hormonal now. You guys are grown men, not high school dudes who don't know how to properly wear a rubber."

"A weenie beanie," corrected Damon.

They all broke up laughing.

"What in the hell were we talking about?" Jameson wanted to know.

"Beats me," answered Coop.

A courier delivered two heavy gun cases, which Kyle instructed be put on one of the couches in the lobby area. He also brought a hot food insulated bag with dinner and a large manilla envelope for Kyle. Their LPO left with the envelope, climbing the stairs two at a time, and promised to return shortly.

While they waited for his meeting to begin, the team spread out the food, expecting to spend the first night in, creating a workup. They knew the location of the place they had to raid. It was a hacienda on a struggling horse ranch not far from their Motel. But Kyle would have the final say after he reviewed their latest intel.

He showed up just as they finished, his arms laden with manilla folders and maps. The team cleared the table, leaving space for Kyle's presentation. He began pulling out pictures of young coeds and several other men, including a priest, while scarfing down a small burrito.

"Rufus Denaro is from Honduras, recently relocated to Baja." Kyle flipped the picture over and tapped the glossy black and white photo. With his mouth full of food, he continued. "He feels like he's struck gold with his little operation of plucking the best-looking tourists and aid workers from their comfortable dorms and putting them to work right away in the sex trade. He apparently tells them, if they'll have sex with him, they'd be helping their fellow workers, keeping them safe. What it is, is rape and abuse. And he's ruthless, so many in the countryside are desperately afraid of him and will avoid any confrontation."

"Do we know how many need rescuing?" asked T.J.

"All of them that we can find. *But*… our prize is really Rufus here. If he's gone, someone else can see to it that the girls are returned home. We're bringing him to Coronado on an outstanding warrant for rape and sex with a minor in Los Angeles, where he escaped detention because of the Sanctuary City law. He absolutely doesn't want to come back to the States, where justice will be served."

"So how many are missing then?" asked Jason.

"And do we know how many are guarding them?" asked Cooper.

"We have two reports. One says eight, the other ten. We have it on good authority that the girls are to be auctioned off online tomorrow. We believe they only have a handful of guards, but the longer they are held, the bigger the team Rufus can assemble, and he'll go after more girls. He's got money, results from his previous ransom-for-hire. He's practiced this for years in Central America. He's just getting started here."

Fredo asked why a larger team wasn't with them.

"We're just supposed to get Rufus. Apparently, that's the deal that was made through our State Department sources."

"Rufus is infringing on someone else's territory, then," Cooper deduced.

"Could be. That's on a need-to-know basis, and I wasn't

given that information. But we can't arrest Mexican nationals. This is *their* country, after all. And the Navy agrees with Mexican authorities it sets a bad precedent to start doing that now, even if it means innocents will be lost this time around. Now, we're not going to let that happen, but we have to keep our eyes on the prize."

"Then we roll out tomorrow night?" asked Tucker.

"Negative. We go tonight."

Coop now understood some of Kyle's concerns and the secret he hadn't divulged to him until he got the final okay. The buzz and whispers amongst the men was normal, but he knew they'd be ready.

Within thirty minutes, the group had geared up. Under cover of darkness, they were instructed to carry light and bring their night vision gear and only one sidearm, which had been issued to each man.

A small tourist van showed up to drop them off closer to the hacienda. They barely had room for their equipment, most having to put their bags on their laps.

The driver was told they were going hunting, but Cooper didn't think he really bought that story. After the van left, he turned to Kyle.

"I notice you didn't tell him when to pick us up, so it's a nice jog back to the motel, right?"

"Exactly." He instructed them to pull down their NV goggles.

The terrain was completely flat. As they approached the property, they could see empty paddocks for various farm animals. One area contained a pair of donkeys, who brayed at the sight of the group. Everyone immediately flattened out on the dirt, listening for signs of guards or lookout, but after several minutes, they were still alone and proceeded closer.

The large ranch house was protected by a stucco perimeter wall with stiff bottlebrush-looking wire and broken bottles on the top of the fence to discourage intruders. Fredo attached his grappling ladder, and Trace and Tucker both removed theirs and attached them. Carefully, the men climbed up the ladder and jumped to the other side. The last man in each group brought the folded ladder with them. They waited and still heard no signs of anyone coming.

Cooper thought it was odd there were no dogs roaming the perimeter. Armando brought out his long gun with the NV scope, carefully scanning to pick up a signature.

"I got nothing," he whispered to Kyle.

Kyle motioned for them to continue. The team split up, encircling the building, while Armando hung back under a tree to be the cover.

Coop always carried a small mirror perfect for peering into buildings or around structures, and he used it to get a look at the living room of the place. There were two lights on, and in the corner, he saw a woman working in the kitchen, cleaning. No one else was visible. He showed Kyle one finger, and then they moved to another window. One by one, the rooms were found to be lit but empty. At the rear of the house, they met up with the other team, who reported two young girls, reading.

Lights appeared from a bus traveling towards the gated entrance. Everyone pushed back their NV scopes and took cover. They watched the driver of the bus get out and opened the gate that wasn't even locked but did lock it behind him after he drove through the entrance. It appeared to be an old white and black prison bus, but there were no notations on it.

It was occupied by several people. When it turned the corner and parked, Coop could make out several armed men and smaller, soft targets: young girls. As they were paraded down the steps, he noticed their wrists were bound and they were pushed along until they bumped into the girl in front of them. A couple of them were crying.

"I count six girls and five armed men," T.J. whispered.

"I'll take those odds," Trace added.

Kyle signaled to encircle the perimeter of the house again. As they split up, another vehicle approached and stopped at the gate, honking three times.

While the girls were shown to the front door, one guard ran to the gate, unlocked it, and allowed the truck driver to enter. Then he hitched a ride with the new visitor. The truck was parked next to the bus. Coop squinted to try to make out the faces of the two men and barely did. Kyle used NV binoculars and studied their gait as they entered.

There was much confusion and discussion. The girls were dressed in a uniform of some kind which consisted of a skirt with tee shirt and then covered by a cloth apron in a dirty light-yellow color. None of them carried a purse, backpack, or suitcase.

"I can't make them out," Coop said as the girls were ushered to rooms in pairs.

"I don't think Rufus is here tonight. We don't have authorization to proceed, dammit."

"The original two girls could belong to the woman working in the kitchen."

"Agreed. Well, shoot. I think we hang out here for a while. Then we head back."

The message was passed around the outside. After nearly thirty minutes, Kyle instructed them to return to the motel.

Even with the jog of some five miles, Coop was so wired up he doubted he'd be able to sleep. And he didn't want to awaken Libby, but he wished he could hear her voice. He wondered how her mother was doing or if Karen had made another appearance.

Just as he'd showed Libby, he began his box breathing, and slowly, he was able to lower his heartbeat. He untucked the sheet and blanket at the bottom to allow his feet to stick out, free from the constraints.

As he lay back, he had a perfect view out one small window. The stars were bright. He took the few seconds to feel gratitude they'd survived another day. He was disappointed there was no firefight, for that's what he was built for, but grateful no one took an injury today. He was alive and healthy. His family was safe. He'd learned after years working on the teams to remember to do this when disappointment began to creep in and mess with him. And then there was the most important part. In his mind, he told Libby he missed her, and he loved her.

He hoped that she was still naked.

CHAPTER 10

Libby was awakened by the telephone. She immediately recognized her dad's phone number.

"You're back?"

"Yes, just landed. Thanks for your message, and I appreciate you arranging the car."

"Sorry, I was going to wait up for you, but it's been a long day again. I went to bed early."

"No, I worry when you have to be out driving late at night by yourself. How's your mom today?"

"She's good. I think she's getting a little tired of going back under, so hopefully that won't happen again for a while. There wasn't time to get back the tissue samples results before I left. I guess they'll have that in the morning."

"Good. Maybe I'll give her a call tonight."

"Even if you wake her up, I think she'd like it. What time do I pick you up?"

"I can get over there on my own, Libby."

"Nope. I insist. You've had a long flight. Sleep in and why don't I pick you up at ten? She should be ready to be discharged by then. I think Dr. Green was hoping you'd be there to help her come home."

"Absolutely. Won't that be a juggle with the kids?"

"They're at Luci and Danny's for their second overnight and, from what I'm hearing, not minding it a bit. But I'll be picking them up from school today, now that you're here."

"Coop's okay?"

"He texted me, yes. He thinks he'll be home in a week."

After they hung up, she lay awake wondering how he'd take the news about his new niece, if in fact Karen was legit. She wished she'd asked more about the mother because she knew her father would want to know.

But then, that's why she wanted to take him over to the hospital.

AUSTIN BROWNLEE WAS out front watering his wife's flowers and shut off the hose when he saw Libby drive up. He grabbed his shoulder satchel, sat in the passenger side of Libby's car, leaned over, and gave her a kiss.

"Nice to have you home, Dad. How did the talk go?"

"They said it went great. Nice change, I was told."

"Your flight was good?"

"They really take care of you on those flights. I slept like a baby. Of course, it was first class."

"Nice, and not at your expense."

"No. I was lucky to be able to get a seat home, since it was three days early."

Libby headed straight for the surgery center. "You got hold of Mom last night?"

"I did, although I don't think she'll remember it. She was

pretty groggy."

"Yes, that's been the case here the last day-plus. The pain meds are strong. From what Dr. Green told me, because there were so many nodes, her sides will hurt the most. She has to sleep on her back."

"She's a trooper. Going to be ordering everyone around soon."

"I've gotten some names from Dr. Green's office. His administrator suggested we can offer a traveling nurse lodging, maybe pick up a pair of them from the registry. They'd be more trained than the regular home health nurses."

"Good idea. Do we have anyone set up for tonight?" he asked.

"Working on it. Started at eight. But we need to know how long the commitment will be, first."

The unspoken issue between the two of them was what kind of treatment was next for Carla. Libby was hoping for more clarity today and was glad her father would be there to ask his questions.

Then she decided to bring up Karen.

"Dad, I have something a little touchy I need to bring up to you."

"About your mom's surgery?"

"No. Nothing to do with that. We had a rather strange visitor day before yesterday. I was over at the house checking on things with Cooper, and a young lady dropped by and said she was Will's daughter."

"Will, my brother? How can that be?"

"She says her mother found out she was pregnant the same

day she received word he'd been killed. Did anyone—your parents or anyone in the family know about this?"

"Never heard a word about it. I have my suspicions, though. There are scammers out there."

"That's what I thought too. I mean, who drops by like that, doesn't try to call or ask first? That in itself is off-putting to me."

"Will wasn't a saint nor a priest. I'm sure he had girlfriends. But no one he was especially close to. I'd be wary." He watched the traffic, sitting still for a few minutes. "She came by the house?"

"She did."

"Very odd. Who is or was her mother?"

"I didn't ask her. We were getting ready to go see Mom after her surgery. Of course, we didn't say anything about that. We were more interested in getting her off the property so we could leave. Sorry. I hope you don't mind. Coop said later he felt a little bad how dismissive we'd been."

"No. I'd have been the same way. But you think her mother is alive?"

"I got the impression, yes."

"Did you tell your mother?"

"Oh God no. Besides, she wasn't in any condition to deal with that."

"Horrible timing."

"That's exactly what Coop said."

"So now I guess I have to get ready for that whole thing. What was she like?"

"She's tall, athletic, said she was coming down to do the

San Diego Marathon. I think she's from Oregon or Washington state. That's where she grew up, anyway. She looks like she could be Coop's twin sister."

"Really! I'll bet that felt strange."

"I was completely unprepared for it. I wasn't very nice to her either."

"Well, one thing at a time. Let's see how our girl is doing, and then we'll deal with that when we have to. Thanks for telling me."

They could hear Carla arguing with one of the nurses from clear down the hall. Libby's dad rolled his eyes and muttered under his breath, "Oh dear."

They stood in the doorway, waiting for the smoke to clear. Carla was perched on the side of the bed, insisting she be allowed to use the restroom. She had already removed her catheter, and urine was spilling in a puddle on the floor.

"Carla, now are you giving these nice ladies a problem?" Libby's dad started.

"Oh, Austin. Tell them. Tell them to get Dr. Green. They won't let me stand up, and I feel fine."

He was immediately over at her side, placing a hand on her shoulder. He let her finish her rant and then leaned over and gave her a kiss.

"Oh, I look horrible. You don't want to see me yet. I was hoping I could brush my hair and put on some lipstick and—"

"Sweetheart, you're fine."

The nurses were whispering between themselves. One tore out of the room. Another began wiping the floor at Carla's feet with a towel from the vanity nearby. The third one stood on the other side, making sure the patient didn't get completely out of bed.

"Look, sweetheart. Let's just lie back and get some instructions from Dr. Green first."

"But I need to pee. I'll wet the bed."

"Go ahead and wet the bed. I don't care about that."

"This is so undignified!" Tears began to stream down her cheeks.

Dr. Brownlee turned to Libby. "Well, I guess that answers the question about how she's feeling."

"She's due for some pain meds. That will settle her down a bit," whispered the nurse. "Come on, Mrs. Brownlee, just lie back a second. We're trying to reach Dr. Green. It all will be sorted in a bit."

Reluctantly they got her back onto the mattress and covered her legs with the blankets. Her arm got tangled in her I.V., which was straightened out and checked. The nurse injected a solution into the tubing.

Libby's dad kept his hand on her shoulder then sat down in the chair Libby slid behind him. "I'd say you've made a rather remarkable recovery, Carla. I can't believe you even want to get up and walk around," he added.

"I'm not sick. It was just surgery. I'm bored to death. I want to get home. I can't sleep here. There's too much noise, and they come in at all times of the night and poke and pick at me. I can't wait to eat real food and get home to my gardens."

"Hi, Mom," Libby said, poking her head around her father's shoulder. "You actually look good."

"You're a pretty little liar!" Carla huffed. "Oh, Austin, go see if they've reached Dr. Green yet. I want to shower and take a pee. I just feel awful."

Before her dad could say anything, Dr. Green himself entered the room.

"What's this I hear about an escaping patient? Do we have to tie you down on the bed, cuff your ankles?"

"Oh, thank heavens. Dr. Green, can't I take a pee?"

Libby's dad and Dr. Green were shaking hands.

"I'm going to ask someone to help you. Austin, you know the rules. You're not allowed to help her. Hospital rules."

"I understand."

"She can sponge you off a bit and give you a clean gown. And you'll be going home today, so hopefully, if you're cooperative, that will cheer you up some." Dr. Green stood to the side as a large nurse disconnected the I.V. and assisted Libby's mom into the bathroom.

With the backdrop of the heated discussion going on in the bathroom, Dr. Green sat on the edge of the bed. "Sit, let's have a brief talk, and then I'll go over it again with her."

Dr. Brownlee took the chair again. Libby chose to stay standing.

"Well, we don't have everything back, but it appears for now we got everything we could get of the cancer. I'm not sure how much Libby has told you, but we had to go in again, and this time I had to scrape very close to the bone, her rib on the right." He demonstrated on himself. "We don't like to see that. But it's something we'll have to watch and hope the radiation and chemo will assist the rest of the way. And we don't know she'll need both or either."

"How long before we know?" Dr. Brownlee asked.

"We want her to heal first. We don't start the regimen until the scar tissue has formed, about a month. At the same time, I don't want to wait too long, so she'll be evaluated before the month is over, and we'll make some decisions on the course of action. We're going to have to be patient, all of us, while we find out the facts of this cancer and what we think her body needs to get rid of it."

"So heal, normal routine, right?" her dad asked.

"Yes. Actually, I call this the honeymoon period. She doesn't feel ill, so she'll want to do things once the pain dulls a bit. We want to keep her strong, eating healthy, keeping the wounds healed, a little bit of exercise, but nothing strenuous."

"I guess she won't be weeding the flower garden, then," added Libby.

"No," Dr. Green chuckled. "But she can sit in a chair and command someone else to do it. I think Carla would like that, actually."

Libby's dad smiled. "That would be me."

"Might be easier if you hired a gardener," Dr. Green suggested.

"They'll be shocked she'll allow them to touch it. But we'll work that out. What is the prognosis?"

"It's advanced stage. I won't lie. Like I told you on the phone, it would have been so much better if we'd caught it sooner. But we're dealing with it now. It all depends on how she tolerates the regimen. And how much is left, like sleeper cells, sort of. But there is a very good chance she'll completely recover. The scan shows no major organs have been invaded, so that's a good thing. We'll monitor her blood and everything carefully, more often at first and then monthly to see how she's doing. As long as it doesn't show up elsewhere, we'll be as aggressive as we can be, give her all the magic we have up our sleeves. But it's a process, and we won't know for sure for several months."

He answered a few more questions and then excused himself to the nurse's station, promising to come back to speak with Carla.

Libby bent over and hugged her dad as he sat. He'd always been the strong one, her rock, the one she relied on. Now she was going to have to be strong for him.

And at the same time, she had Cooper and his mission and the kids, of course. As she stood up, ready to greet her mother emerging from the restroom, she knew that the next few weeks were going to be full. She was a daughter, a wife, a sometimes-single parent when Coop was away, a counsellor.

Her hat rack was full.

CHAPTER 11

COOP SPENT THE morning fiddling with his drone. He'd made improvements over the past several months in his free time, including installing a tiny remote hook that could release a small package. It was strong enough to hold a cell phone, spider phone location device, small explosive charge, or flash bomb, even a listening device dropped into landscaping. Where the object landed wasn't an exact science, and he was working on improving that some. Right now, it was as simple as a clip that held and then released. Off and on. Strictly binary.

But he was rather proud of it, ever since the first day he saw her and flew her on a test run over ten years ago. His love for his little bird, over all the others in his collection he'd obtained afterward, was enormous. The drone was a part of his family now, and he felt a sense of responsibility for its protection and care.

Several of the men went into town proper, completing their cover, noticing the groups and looking for bad guys they'd seen before. T.J. and Armando stayed behind with Coop. Kyle went in with the larger group to pick up a fifteen-passenger van just in case a partial rescue of the girls was needed. He'd communicated his distrust of the local tourist vans and taxi transports for hire, especially worried about a tipoff to Rufus Denaro or his men.

T.J. was trying to locate the auction and had been given several frequencies to study. There was an offshore radio station they'd been told had recently picked up a television signal.

He'd located one station that had a weak visual signal, playing Mexican pop tunes to still pictures of villages, fiestas, and some of the beautiful scenery, including the beaches and fishing tours.

And then the screen became live.

"Hola, we got something coming in," yelled T.J.

"Can you record it?" asked Coop.

"Sure, can try, but I'm going to video it on my cell. Get me my charger, Armani," T.J. demanded.

They watched T.J.'s computer screen display a line of girls, all dressed in identical white gowns, while the background announcer was saying something T.J. and Coop didn't understand in Spanish.

When Armando arrived with the charger, he translated while hooking up the adapter and charger for T.J.'s cell.

"They say the auction will only last for ten minutes. They are instructing the interested parties call their contact person and give their bid. The winning bid number will be posted after the bidding is closed. Holy shit, they're only allowing a minute each. Sixty seconds to purchase a girl, goddammit," Armando swore.

“This must be coming from the house,” Coop gasped. “I’m gonna get the drone.”

The announcer was giving details of the girls. Armando recited age ranges. At one point he told the audience they were healthy, from the United States, and transport outside the U.S. would cost the bidder extra and wasn’t included in the bid price.

“A shipping and handling fee,” T.J. swore. “These people have the nerve.”

Coop slotted the wing inside the body of his drone, attached the little video feed to the nose cone, and then flipped a tiny black switch, starting the whir of the near-silent motor. He ran outside, set the controller on a chair, extended his arm back with his fingers clutching the belly of the device, and then ran forward, pushing the drone out of his hands and launching it into the sky. He grabbed the controller, immediately adjusted the trajectory to get higher, then aimed it at the ranch.

He watched the monitor as it traveled over the flat prairie and then gained altitude. Within three minutes, it was over the ranch, and he slowly spiraled it down to within two hundred feet of the rooftop.

Calling through the open door to the lobby area where T.J. and Armando were, Coop asked for a status.

Armando appeared at his side, watching the monitor. “They are in a room with a corrugated back wall. Is there a shed or building made of metal anywhere on the property perhaps?”

Back and forth, the pictures showed wooden and stucco structures, some with metal roofing, and some with tile, but nothing that looked like a shed.

Then Coop spotted a shipping container. The sides were heavily grooved with two large metal doors opening outward. One of those doors was open, revealing a dark space inside.

"I'm going to see if I can get down lower," Coop said.

"It's starting. Auction's starting," they heard T.J.'s voice from the lobby. "Armani, call Kyle."

As Coop swept lower, the opening to the shipping container became larger. He could barely see a light from inside but didn't want to get too low so that he avoided detection. When he turned up the magnification, the picture became so pixilated it was not recognizable. He gave a wide-angle view of the whole complex and showed the location of the container with respect to the ranch house itself.

Armando had just hung up with Kyle, who indicated he'd be back at their base within thirty minutes. He directed Coop and T.J. to upload their recordings to the Naval Intelligence Task Force in Coronado.

The bird recorded that the white bus used last night to transport the girls was still parked in its same location. But several newer all-terrain vehicles and trucks had arrived at the complex, and nearly a dozen other people were milling about, some going in and out of the storage container.

Coop attempted to let the drone swoop lower but spotted a helicopter making its way to the complex from the north. He sent the bird to a higher elevation to avoid detection then hovered and enlarged the image. The unmistakable frame of Rufus Denaro stepped out of the helicopter and convened with several others who had gathered around him. Then the whole group entered the shipping container.

Kyle and the other Team members arrived in a large white passenger van. His LPO ran over to Cooper.

"You sending this up yet?"

"Yup. I think T.J.'s sending stuff too. You should see that feed, if it's still there."

"I plan to. So you have the whole complex charted?"

"Even the road leading up to it, all the way until the next structure. Things heated up with that helicopter landing. Got a good look at Rufus firsthand before he went inside."

Kyle watched the view of the whole complex, counting vehicles and manpower.

"Coronado is going to be thrilled with that footage. How many do you count?"

"There are six or seven inside the container right now, another dozen we can see, plus whoever is in the house, but I'm guessing we got short of twenty. More likely fifteen."

"That's not bad. You see anything that indicates they'll be loading the girls up?"

"I'm guessing that's next. I think they'd wait until cover of darkness. Although it was pretty bold to land that helicopter right in the middle in broad daylight."

"I don't think they know they're being watched. Sure would like to know where they got their buyers from." After a few minutes, Kyle asked another question. "You have a few more minutes left on the battery?"

"I'd like to bring her in soon. Been about forty minutes."

"Okay, let's get her charged up and ready for a night surveillance. Good job, Coop."

After Kyle left, Coop let the drone scale up then fly East, just in case someone was watching. He brought her home with a fairly soft landing, just scraping the bottom of her belly in some soft dirt. A cloud of dust descended everywhere.

Coop put the controller back in the cushioned case, leaving the body of the drone on a table outside the lobby area while he went in search of a cleaning rag.

Inside, everyone was hunched around the replay of the auction T.J. was airing. Armando and Fredo were translating parts, which sounded more like a children's pageant or a game show than what it really was. The whole thing only lasted about twelve minutes.

At the end, there was no contact information, no phone number or name of any company or event sponsor—nothing to identify themselves in any way. The feed announcer said "adios," and it went back to the music and still photos from before.

Coop was stunned at the speed of the operation and the efficiency with which lives were being bartered. It was a simple system, using a low frequency T.V. channel, hacking into it, and then handing the controls back over to the station. It wasn't obvious if they were cooperating or were being used.

The complicated part was the exchange of money and transport of the girls to their desired destination. It allowed Rufus and his gang to offload their contraband quickly, get their money, and move on to the next sale. If the SEALs could find the station and stop the signal, they'd just hack into another one and do a surprise popup there, Coop thought.

Kyle told everyone to take a break, catch some rest, and be

prepared to move out at nightfall. Once again, he was waiting for instructions from the Headshed.

Sitting in the mid-day sun, wiping down the sleek plastic drone, Coop used the bit of quiet time to meditate as he stroked her body and rubbed out a couple of scratches left on the underside of her. The craziness of the town was a long distance away. It felt like the way corn fields in Nebraska were in the early summer, when the stalks came up to his shoulder and all he could hear was the sound of the wind blowing through the long green spears. Knowing what he now knew about how quickly the tornado could come swooping through, ruin three generations of work on a family farm he'd expected to inherit and help run one day, he felt that quiet before the storm now.

There were a lot of things blowing in the breeze. Libby's mom and how that would affect Libby and the kids, the potential new addition to the family, the changes afoot at the border with such a heavy concentration of criminal activity always present but now coming on like a firehose, so close to the land that he'd made an oath to save and protect. He began to see the cycle as a never-ending story, some huge mission that could never really be fully accomplished, just chipped away at.

He'd always understood there was only one part of the game of war they could control, and that was what they did as a cohesive unit. But now they were going to have to train for a different enemy. And just like people in South America, Africa, and the Middle East, there were far more innocents hurt than the actual bad guys. The trick was always to control the bad guys without costing innocent lives.

While it was frustrating to work this way, he had to rely on his training and trust the tasks that were given him. Some of those were flawed, based on faulty intel either purposely misleading or sometimes just resulting from an oversight. But these were new rules being developed, and they didn't have decades working on their systems. Even the Coast Guard's mission changed dramatically in the last twenty years with the influx of drug trade and the lucrative human trafficking going on today. It was just as much a war as any other that was being fought. But in war, more people died, especially civilians. This special warfare was devised to diminish that cost of treasure.

Were they doing too good a job at it? Did they make it look too easy? He knew the public expected the SEALs could do anything. But the more the problem grew and the more there was sympathy and tolerance to the drug trade in the U.S. and a desire to put blinders on when it came to the human trafficking trade, the more difficult it was to fight this enemy. He hoped that his country didn't all of a sudden lose the appetite to fight evil.

But it was something Coop worried about every day, just like all the other brothers he worked with. The pattern of bloodshed and then giving up the battles and moving on, leaving so much loss behind, was now openly discussed, and he sensed the general public's appetite for conflict away from home was being swayed by the conflicts at home.

For the first time in his career, Coop saw that perhaps the greatest threat his country faced was at home. And maybe it had been there all along.

He wasn't into being a hero. He just wanted to keep as many people safe as he could. He hoped people with heart and faith ran the plays. But for now, he could continue to carry the ball. The saving grace for him was that he got to play an elite game with some of the greatest men on the planet.

His drone was clean. She was smooth and just as beautiful as ever, and she was far more to him than plastic, batteries, springs, and wiring.

She was his spear.

CHAPTER 12

COOP'S CALL CAME in while Libby and her dad were loading Carla into the car.

"I'm sure you can hear all the commotion going on. I hate to make you call back, but I'd love to talk and can't right now."

Carla screamed as her husband helped her into the front seat. The orderly was retracting the wheelchair a little too soon, and she slid into the seat at an awkward angle.

"I got you," Coop said. "I'll give you about thirty minutes? That good enough?"

"Perfect. We're headed to the house as soon as we're done here, and they can take it from there. We have someone who is going to stay tonight to help Dad out."

"I'll bet you miss the kids," he said. "But hey, talk to you in a few. Don't strain yourself, and be careful!"

"Love you, Coop."

"Back at you."

Carla called out, "Tell him I said come home safe."

"Did you hear?" Libby asked.

"I did. How could I not? Don't tell her this, but I'm glad you're the one doing that. I'd rather be here."

Libby covered for him. "He says he loves you too, Mom." She heard Coop laughing as he hung up.

Satisfied she'd done everything she could, and with Ynez and the nurse on hand, she hugged her dad one more time and escaped to the safety of her car. She waited until she'd turned the corner before she took a deep breath in and then out, suddenly feeling free from the burden. It wasn't something she was proud of, but she knew from her counseling training it was normal to want to escape the responsibilities of caring for an ill family member. And it was healthy to get breaks, enlist help, and not to let the situation overwhelm, which it did in many cases.

She couldn't wait to see Will and Gillian again.

She stopped to get some fresh pasta and marinara sauce from the Italian deli on the way home, along with some favorite cookies the kids liked and Mama Leone's famous garlic bread. It would be a feast for them, and she'd sit back with her glass of wine and listen to the stories, some of which she knew she'd regret hearing.

Cooper still hadn't called, so she got the mail, unloaded her groceries, and then kicked off her running shoes before she set up the food prep. Her feet hurt from being laced up and inactive. She poured herself a big glass of ice water and sat on the patio to give herself a few minutes of listening to the waves before she had to get the kids at school.

And then he called.

"I know why I married you," she whispered, touching the rim of the glass with her forefinger.

"I definitely know why I married you. I can't think of anyone else on the planet who could get me so excited dirty-talking on the phone."

"It's not dirty-talking."

"It is the way I do it, honey. It's definitely dirty. But that's okay. You can call it anything you like."

She allowed that familiar zing down her spine to complete loosen her nerves. "I love how you do that."

"What?"

"Make me feel good. How did I get so lucky?"

"You stood there with your long legs, that pout on your face, and challenged me, telling me I wasn't welcome, and I could see already you'd surrendered to me."

"Right there?"

"Right there. In your parent's foyer. You were mine the instant you let me in the front door."

"That's funny, because you didn't let on at all."

"Because you wanted me to fight for you. You wanted me to come crashing over your little white picket fence and take you in my arms and make you my woman, Libby. I suddenly had a new mission in life, and you were it."

"I never knew you made up your mind so fast."

"You know me, honey. When I'm done, I'm done. I was cooked. I was ready the second after you looked at me. You remember what you said that got me so tickled?"

"Something about bringing up the past?" she proffered.

"No. You said, '*We don't speak military here.*' You remember that?"

"Now that you mention it, I do."

"I knew I wanted to teach you all my favorite Navy cuss

words, and some other ones. I wanted you to whisper, 'Roger that' and 'report for duty, sailor' and all kind of other things. And you were a fast learner, too."

"You are a good teacher, Cooper." She was actually getting wet just playing with him on the phone.

"I think I'm coming home early."

She could tell it was a tease.

"You're chicken to."

"Don't tempt me too much."

"What are you doing now?"

Coop sighed and then began. "Well, I thought about you while I was rubbing down my drone. She has a smooth body, just like yours. Her curves are subtle, cool to the touch, but when I flip her switch, she quivers and purrs in my ear, just like you do."

"So you had your way with your drone, did you? You be careful. They'll toss you from the Navy if you do unmentionable things to the equipment."

"No, ma'am. My equipment I'm saving for your equipment. I'm gonna get all geared up, pumped up, and ready to plunder. I'm gonna hook up to your gear and, sweetheart, we're gonna fly somewhere you've never been. Maybe we'll get lost. How would that be? Just get away from everything, at least for a few minutes…"

"Hours?"

"Yes, hours are better. Remember those contests we used to have, how many times we could do it?"

"How could I forget? I had a hard time walking around after."

"I had a hard time getting my pants on in those days. Darned buttons just wouldn't stay put together."

"And you'd bump into things…"

"Oh, you should talk. Remember the goose egg you got on your forehead when you ran into the side of the door?"

"Don't remind me."

"Your dad took me aside and made sure I didn't lay a hand on you."

"He never told me that."

"He was just checking."

"So what did you tell him?"

"I said we were having one of those contests again. And he blushed. I've never seen him blush that way since."

"I can only imagine what he said to my mom."

"I'm sure he used it, somehow." Cooper chuckled. "Anyway, sweetheart, I'm sitting here and looking over the flat plain and thinking of how much I miss you. Miss the kids. But I'm safe right now."

"When does the action start?" She knew she wasn't supposed to ask that question but was happy to needle him further.

"When I get home, Libby. We'll dance to Mariachi music, and you can have one strawberry margarita."

"Just one?"

"Maybe two, if you're real good."

"I can be real good."

"Oh, don't you know it! I'm counting on that."

"So do you have anything big and important to tell me?" She laughed into the phone and, then with her sexiest voice, added, "Especially if it's big."

"Honey, I'm going to embarrass myself now. I've got something big for you, and I hope you dream about it every night, because the longer I'm away, the bigger it will get."

"Oh my!"

"Cooper, the name's Cooper. Say my name the way you do when you come, honey."

"Cooper," she breathed into the phone. "Make me come, Cooper. I need it."

All she could hear was heaving breathing on the other end.

"Thank you, sweetheart. This was such an important conversation. I just needed to connect with you. God, you're the best, Libby."

She was blushing. He was so free to show how much he cared for her. She'd thought at first he was so quiet, but it was the depth of his feelings that eventually snagged her and swept her off her feet.

"I hope they don't monitor these calls when you're over there."

"Not here. And who cares? We're crazy for each other. I'm not ashamed of it."

"Me neither. I hope it will always be that way, Coop."

"Trust me, it will be."

Libby checked her phone for the time. "I would love to sit here for another hour and do dirty talk with you, but I have to go pick up your little clones, Coop. The kids we made together when we were having so much fun."

He chuckled again. "Okay then. You're excused. Give them a hug from me. And please, sleep naked again. I liked it last night."

"You sent your drone over to check up on me?"

"Wish I could have. But no, she was off doing something else. You take care, and I'll try to call tomorrow."

"Thanks for the feels."

"I've only just begun, sweetheart."

"I feel it already. Love you, Coop. Come back to me soon."

SHE CHUCKLED ALL the way over to the kids' school. She sat in the line of cars that snaked around the front of the campus, all parents waiting to pick up their children. Finally, she saw Gillian walking with a girlfriend just as Will came swooping up behind them, passing them up, and claiming the front seat of the car, which was always the prize.

Gillian complained but was the first to lean over the back seat and give Libby a kiss on her cheek. "I'm so happy to see you today. When Luci told us you'd be here, I was ecstatic!"

"I thought you liked it over at Luci and Danny's."

"Those boys are awful! They stick me with Chester now that Griffin is bigger. One of these times, I'm going to put Ali's slingshot down the garbage disposal," she said in a huff.

Will objected. "She was a brat. But she's got a secret."

"I do not. That's a lie!"

Will wasn't going to be deterred. "She told Griffin she liked Ali."

Libby's eyes grew large, surprised at the reveal. She didn't want to embarrass her daughter further so kept mum but looked at Gillian's guilty face in the rearview mirror.

When they made eye contact, her daughter offered an excuse.

"I did it so he'd leave me alone. He plays rough. Too rough sometimes."

"That's because he plays like a—"

"Stop it right now, Will. That's not nice, and I want you to stop it. Gillian, if he plays too rough, you tell him so, and if he won't stop, then you tell Luci or Danny. You know they won't put up with it. Your dad or I wouldn't either."

"Okay," Gillian said quietly. She'd been embarrassed.

Libby knew what she was feeling. "Can I tell you a story a teacher of mine told me? She told me that, when boys really like a girl and they are just getting used to the idea of playing or being friends with a girl, they often pretend they don't like them because they don't know what to do. It came up because one boy at school threw plums at me, and it stained my dress. I went to my teacher, and she told me that."

"Did he get in trouble for it?" asked Will.

"He sure did, and he deserved it. But after that, we became friends, kind of. He stopped being that way. We were friends for many years."

"Was he your boyfriend?" asked Gillian.

"No. But he was a friend. Years later, we went to a dance together. He was a nice boy, after all."

Libby wasn't sure if her message had left any impression on either of the kids, because they drove all the way home without another word.

And then over spaghetti and French bread, she told them about their grandmother and her surgery.

CHAPTER 13

"OKAY, GENTS." KYLE gathered everyone together. "We have a change of plans. Our goal is still to get Rufus Denaro, but now that we have evidence of the human trafficking, we're authorized to do a rescue if Denaro isn't there. We have more than enough evidence to prove a crime is being committed here, but it's still not our jurisdiction. We aren't allowed to do anything but extract him and conduct a rescue of any American or suspected-American hostages. And since the video feed announcer nicely said they were Americans, well, that sort of settles it."

Coop had a feeling the upper levels of the Navy would agree to more than an abort mission this time, and thankfully, he was right.

They were told there were satellite photos being taken all day long, and Coop's drone shots revealed the container registration number, and it was traced to a cargo ship that had docked in Cabo a few weeks ago.

It didn't take Coop long to figure out they might have plans for using cargo containers like this one for transport overseas or even up into Canada. The containers could be trading both sides, importing drugs and weaponry. He could see this little cabal was just getting started, and they had big plans, having pushed aside several local groups. To make matters worse, the SEALs had helped to weaken two other cartels in the area, dismantling one and doing surveillance for a joint US-Mexican operation that removed all the members of another family.

Cooper figured Denaro was some local's pain in the ass, so the intel had been brought to his team to help with extraction, thereby eliminating the problem.

They were to gear up, have some chow, and then move out as soon as it was dark.

Kyle added, "This time, we'll be going in style, motorized each way."

He later explained the footage collected in Coronado showed another trail that wound up closer to the ranch, where a van could park in a thicket of small bushes and be hidden from the trail itself. It had been a prior smuggler's route, but the new group might not be yet aware of it.

"So we caught some luck then. That what you're saying?" Coop asked him.

"Not knowing what the condition those ladies will be in, I'd say it's a godsend."

That was always an unknown in an operation: the condition of the hostages. Some of them might be drugged, and some of them may have been abused in varying degrees. It was best to plan for the worst and then have it turn out easier.

Coop hoped there were no kids in the group. He had even more difficulty tamping down his anger when that occurred.

But he stayed mentally prepared.

"You thinking they'll move them out tonight? Perhaps bring more in tomorrow?" Coop asked Kyle as they checked their pockets for the trip.

"You gotta admit that was a little high profile, and it might have alerted attention, especially from their rivals. So I'm thinking yeah. Move their valuable merchandise out ASAP, in the dark. Wouldn't be the first time one group went to all the trouble to kidnap or steal only to have another cartel take it from them and be the ones to actually profit."

"Was the Headshed surprised how ballsy they were? Right on a low frequency T.V. station and probably right under someone else's nose."

"They didn't say. But it had to have attracted attention since sometimes buyers will buy from anyone who has the product. All it takes is someone sour over not getting their bid in to spill it to someone else who can help them get even."

About eight-thirty, they took their seats in the van and headed south, Kyle driving with Coop up front. His LPO turned to him, "You brought the drone, right? Outfitted with night scopes?"

"Sure did. She's got a fresh charge, and I double checked the camera and the feed earlier.

The desert trail they were on looked like the surface of Mars. Small rocks encrusted in clumps of mud were everywhere. There wasn't any grass or outcroppings except in little divots in the surface of the plain where there might be a spring. Even out here in the desert, soda cans and plastic bags littered the area, perhaps blown there from miles away. No recent tire tracks marred the dusty trail, and Kyle drove slowly, with just his parking lights on to distract anyone's attention who might be watching from the foothills beyond.

"How's Libby's mom?" Kyle asked him.

"Better. She came home today. Austin got home last night so Libby's got the kids and got a night off."

"You might call that a night off, but I don't."

"Come on, Kyle, those kids of yours love you."

"Oh, they do. That's because they can pull things over on me they can't get away with Christy. She's pretty tough."

"I've seen it. She did a good job on the cruise. She and Libby make a good team. Funny how the women have no problem handling them," Coop said.

"You've got two. I have three. Big difference."

Coop laughed. "Soon to be four. Don't forget about that!"

"How could I ever? And shut up. I don't want anyone else to know about it."

"Um, Kyle, they know. They're studying names to give you. Names you're gonna ignore."

Kyle approached the small thicket of bushes and a tree split by a lightning strike. He angled the van so that the greenery hid it completely from the trail they'd just been on.

"Get a couple guys to go cover up those tracks, will you, Coop?"

"On it." He directed Damon and Jason to drag an old beach towel he found in the back of the van over the dusty evidence of their passing.

The gear was unloaded. Since Coop had the drone, he transferred his medic pack to T.J. to add to his. After a couple of last-minute adjustments of load and weight, they were ready to head up the little mound to the ranch.

The sky had a scattering of clouds that moved across the stars and the nearly full moon, changing the landscape from bright moonlight to black hole, so it played havoc with their NVRs. Coop flipped his up and relied on his regular sight. He noticed Armando did the same.

Coop hooked in one of the grappling ladders and slowly inched to the top of the stucco perimeter fencing, the large wings of his drone spread out to the sides as if he was a dragonfly. Someone made such a comment and was quickly shushed.

Armando was on another ladder and used his scope to search the campus. They heard music coming from the house. Two of the bedrooms appeared to have lights on. The only voices they heard were male.

He and Armando both landed at the same time on the other side, and Armando found a small olive tree to climb where he could reach the roof of a corrugated shed and began setting up for sniper cover.

The others made it over while Coop prepared the drone to launch. Fredo passed out several Invisios, making sure Coop and Armando got one, as well as he and Kyle.

They all hit the ground when they heard the sounds of boots walking nearby. They were close enough to see the guards faces as one man lit a match between them and they each took a smoke. Their conversation was staccato and hard to hear, but Fredo translated what he could.

"Talking about the girls and how pretty they are. One of

them is wondering if the new boss would allow them to earn credits to perhaps buy himself a bride. What a dickwad. There are a pair of twins in the group, and they both went to the same buyer, the other one says. Sick fuck. One of them is getting ten thousand pesos and the other only eight thousand. These sound like new hires. Not part of the regular crew," Fredo finished.

The two finished their cigarettes and then joined a group inside one of the large main rooms of the house. A sliver of remnant smoke traveled toward Coop, nearly making him sneeze.

"I'm all set, Kyle," Coop reported, holding his drone in front of him, facing downhill toward the town of Cabo itself.

"Let her fly," came the answer.

Coop's height always gave his birds a boost when he was tossing them. He aimed it in an arc, knowing it would soon level off and swoop downwards for a few seconds until the controller could be managed. Keeping it low on the horizon also kept it from being visible from anyone who might be standing on the ranch house's roof or on a nearby knoll.

He adjusted the green picture on the screen to get a clearer focus, careful to read height and direction. A small plane was flying overhead, on its way to making a remote landing in the desert somewhere. Coop didn't think his drone was in danger of being spotted.

He turned the bird around in a huge circle, coming back over the house from nearly four hundred feet, and then used the camera lens to zoom closer before he lowered his height another hundred feet or so. He could see the whole complex on the screen. Heat signatures showed up in a couple of larger clusters, one outside the ranch on the far side, where there was a patio and pool area. There seemed to be a gathering of a dozen or so individuals.

On the east side of the house perimeter, another covered patio area had a cluster of people sitting in rows with others appearing to be guards or sentries moving up and down between the rows.

Kyle looked over his shoulder at the pictures. He called Trace and Jameson to search out the group of suspected hostages and report a count. He sent two others, Fredo and Jason, to surveille the larger group on the patio. He instructed Tucker to go be a bad boy.

"Sir?"

"Haven't you ever wanted to do in some expensive tires on expensive vehicles?"

"Not really, Kyle."

"Never mind," Kyle beamed. "Go stab the shit out of those tires enough to make them not useable."

"How many of them?"

"All of them. You can leave the bus alone. We'd need Fredo for that. Tell me when you're done and wait to join Fredo and Jason. They'll be southwest of the patio."

"On my way."

"Fredo, be ready with some diversion. Can you set up a remote small IED?"

"Sure. I got flash bombs too."

"No, I don't want anything thrown unless we have to. Just something to get your group to take cover and come over to investigate. I think there's a small pickup on that side. Use that."

"As in waste it?"

"Nah, just break the glass." He chuckled. "Of course, you can waste it, Frodo. Make it count."

Within seconds, Fredo and Jason had disappeared into the night.

Coop had an idea that sprang into his head. He'd been watching someone going and coming from the house from his overhead perch. "They're entertaining. Perhaps they're expecting guests? I don't think all these people over here are bad guys. Some may be customers."

"Good observation." Kyle whispered instructions to the scouts to sort out, if they could, who was military and who was a visitor or customer. Fredo also confirmed he'd set up the explosive charge.

Within seconds, they had the outside count. Tucker had ruptured most of the tires on the expensive Land Rovers and Jeeps in the driveway. "Can you send them a message on the feed, Coop?"

"Sure. Got one line."

"Six civilians, eleven girls, ten military males," he dictated. Coop typed in the words on his screen.

Damon approached Kyle, "If Armani can cover me, I'll get a closer look inside the windows. Perhaps there will be more inside. Should I check?"

"That's a good idea, Damon. Off with you." He instructed Armando to carefully watch over Damon, who was now the one closest to the enemy.

"Copy that," Armando answered. "I can easily hit anyone who wants to fuck him over."

Damon's heavy breathing came over the com. "We got two fully armed guards sitting at the kitchen table. The cook is preparing something, and a pair of young girls—they look very young, Kyle—bringing trays of food out to the patio guests. I'm going to slip around the back and see if I can see inside one of the bedrooms."

"Watch yourself. Everyone stand ready. If he kicks a hornet's nest, that's the go signal."

Kyle asked Coop to quickly bring the drone down for a closer view of the audience on the south side patio by the pool and switch off the NVR. "I want to see if we got enough light to really make an identification."

Landscape lighting interfered with some of the projection, but gradually, every one of the faces were mapped, charted, and sent up the command. They hoped there were some really big fish present who would rue the day they attended this party. But there was still no sign of Rufus in that crowd. Coop guessed he wouldn't be in the back guarding the hostages either. He was unaccounted for or not present.

"Okay, Coop. Shut her down. We're ready to move. Get ready for my mark, everyone."

Coop stored the bird in the padded zipper bag, added it to his pack, and indicated he was ready.

"And we have two more girls, oh shit. I didn't want to see this."

"Cut the chatter, Damon."

"Sex by force. Two on two, and it's not consensual."

Coop knew what that meant. Every man on the team knew it, too, and they would all have the same determination and resolve.

"Damon, your job is to rescue those two any way you can, got it?"

"Yessir."

"On my mark. It's go at the blast. Ready, Fredo?"

"It's showtime," Fredo repeated.

The blast lifted the pickup into the air nearly ten feet. Examining it, Coop figured out why. The truck had no motor to weigh it down. But the firebomb ignited a storage building that must have contained some flammable material because they got an unexpected gift of a second explosion bigger than the first.

The group on the patio scattered, several men running for their vehicles. But mass confusion descended as the guards didn't know which direction to fire without hitting some of the hostages or customers. One by one, the team overcame and disabled all the combatants, usually delivering a non-lethal shot to the thigh or groin area. Firepower was removed. Kyle and Cooper ran to the east side and assisted Trace and Jason with the girls. Damon made short work of the two men inside the bedroom and brought the girls out the back to join the larger group.

The last act of resistance was the two armed guards inside the house. One took the cook at gunpoint to her head. The other grabbed one of the young girls and exited out the front door into the courtyard, for some strange reason.

As they led the girls down the side trail to their waiting

van, Coop saw Armani's save, hitting both guards in the middle of the forehead in two perfect shots a split second apart. Both men fell and released their captives.

Several of the vehicles stormed the gate and drove off, even with ruined tires. One had difficulty maneuvering a turn and landed on its side.

For now, they had managed to sneak into the thicket and disappear without a trace. But Coop knew that, as soon as word got out about the raid, the whole place was about to become an anthill.

His only regret as he climbed aboard the van, standing in the center aisle which allowed all the young girls to have a seat, was that damned slippery Rufus. He knew they'd be tasked with cleaning that up in the future.

He had to put all that out of his mind and tend to his patients, the two girls who had been raped. T.J. was already caring for the first one.

She sat staring out the window at the fire, her arms about her body as she rocked, trying to keep herself warm.

Coop found a foil blanket and wrapped it around her. She didn't seem to notice.

"Hey, we're here to help. Can you tell me your name?"

She stared at him. Vacant. Damaged.

"We're the good guys, honey. I'm here to check you out. Where did he hurt you?"

She pulled aside the foil blanket to show him her wound. Her lap was stained with blood.

CHAPTER 14

AFTER DROPPING THE kids off at school, Libby headed to her parents' house to check on her mom. On the way, she called Neil.

"Hey, sis. How's she doing?"

"They had a second surgery day before yesterday, and it appears, for now, they have no plans to go in again. But so far, they're hoping they got everything. Almost impossible to know until they get a scan in a few days or weeks. I'm not sure."

"So she had both—?"

"Yes, she had both breasts removed and most of the lymph nodes under both arms. That's because it had already spread. We're hoping it didn't spread farther. She's supposed to heal first. Then they'll start with another regimen. Not sure whether that's just chemo or radiation or both."

"I see. How is she? I mean, is she in pain?"

"Nothing the meds can't handle. She needs them. Doesn't mean she's enjoying it. But she's very upbeat, starting to boss everyone around, which we think is a good sign."

"I'm just so conflicted. Don't know if a visit will make it

better or worse. Does she want to see us?"

"Neil, I'd say that doesn't matter. I'm not going to suggest anything. Do what you feel like doing. We all know it costs money to fly a whole family out. I can't pay for it, Neil, and Dad hasn't offered, so it's on you."

"Oh, I wouldn't ask them. Not about the money, Libby. Everyone gets me wrong all the time about that."

Says my brother who was always too busy to come visit, slammed at work for their wedding anniversary.

"Do what you feel like doing. Do what feels right."

"Maybe me and Marsha should come together. Might be a nice couple of days in San Diego. I always love coming home. I can leave the kids with friends of theirs for a few days no problem."

"Yes, I think that would be very nice. I think they'd both like to see you. And Marsha."

"Let me get something arranged, and I'll let you know."

"I have a couple SEAL families who do Airbnb bedrooms if you want something a little less expensive than a regular hotel. Let me know if you need that."

"Oh, thank you. No, Marsha likes room service, champagne on demand, lots of TV channels, movies, you get the drill."

Libby could imagine it quite well. She wasn't keen on the idea of her brother staying with anyone she knew from the community, either, but she offered anyway.

CARLA WAS OUTSIDE on her rear patio drinking coffee and watching Ynez pick flowers in her garden. "Hi, dear," she greeted Libby with a kiss on her cheek when she bent down.

"How are you feeling this morning? You look great."

"Not bad, really. I made poor Austin sleep in the guest room. I was up and down all night. We have a couple people helping, a sister and brother from Fiji, and they took turns each staying part of the night. And boy do they insist on me drinking tons of water, so of course I had to pee all night long. But all the swelling from the surgery is going down, except in my arms and hands."

"That's good. Means your body is flushing out all the toxins."

"You think that's it? Well, I do feel more like myself, even with the meds. But thank god for them."

"What time do they get here?"

"Around four. Ynez cooks dinners for all of us, and then after dinner, either Austin or Annie, that's the sister, helps me shower, and I get ready for bed. And then her brother comes and relieves her around two and stays until after breakfast. They're both licensed, so they can give shots, my meds, and have communication with Dr. Green if they need to. I really like the arrangement."

"That must have been the service Dr. Green spoke about."

"Yes, through him. Anyway, Austin is getting ready for the office upstairs if you want to see him."

"Let me hop up there and talk to him for a sec. Then I'll be right back down."

"You like this, Mrs. Carla?" Ynez held a small bouquet of sweet peas, roses, and snap dragons.

Libby climbed the stairs, anxious to talk to her dad.

"In here, sweetie. How are the kiddos?" He was in the bathroom straightening his tie.

"Here, let me do that." Carla always insisted on doing her dad's tie every morning, and now he claimed he didn't know how anymore.

"Thank you. That's what I needed."

His warm eyes, tanned face, and light silver hair made him movie star attractive. The thing Libby liked the most about him was that he was completely oblivious to it. That also led to his attractiveness.

She broached the subject of Karen.

"Have you told Mom about your new niece? Or should I say supposed niece?"

"God no. Not yet. I think I'll wait and see if she reaches out again. No need disturbing Carla if I don't have to."

"Okay. Well, just let me know if you want me to talk to Mom about it. She might not take it well if it's just sprung on her."

"I'm sure Ynez won't let anyone in here unless one of us is home, so no worries there. The more I think about it, the surer I am that it was a possible scam. And, if she's real, we'll find out soon enough."

"Okay, I'll leave that in your capable hands. So you're off to the office."

"I have some appointments I agreed to take that I'd re-scheduled for the trip. So I'm kind of bunched up. But only three-quarters of the day. I'll be home early."

"Good. I think getting back to a normal routine will be exactly what she needs."

"What about you?"

"Same here. Coop comes back soon, I hope, but no word yet. Will has a soccer tournament this weekend, and I agreed to run the snack bar for the club. Gillian wants to help."

"What time is the game?"

"They play four minimum, unless they go to the championship round. Starts eight on Saturday. I think the next one is ten. And then it depends on who they play after. Sunday morning, they are guaranteed one game, so it could be over quick."

"Text me your schedule, and I'll see if I can stop by."

They began coming down the stairs, her father following her. "Sounds like the brother and sister nurses are working out with mom. She seems to like them."

"Very lovely people. They consider it their calling, to heal the sick."

Libby had heard that their culture valued the experience of death, too, but didn't want to mention it to her dad.

Dr. Brownlee said good-bye to his wife, hugged Libby, and left the house. Ynez brought Libby a coffee while she sat with her mom.

"I'd like a refresher too, Ynez," her mom called out.

"*Si*, no problem. I'll be right out with a fresh cup."

"I spoke with Neil, and he's thinking just he and Marsha should come out and visit with you. They're working on plans, and they'll let me know."

"I guess I better bury the hatchet with Marsha, shouldn't I? When you're lying in bed and waiting to hear if you're going to be okay or if you're on death's door, funny how life takes on a new perspective. I sure don't want to check out without making amends to her."

"You're not going to check out, Mom. That's not going to happen."

"You speak for yourself. No one gets out of this life alive, right?"

"Right. But what I meant was, don't be too pessimistic. I thought you said you were going to beat this thing."

"I said that all right. I've developed a healthy respect for this beast inside me. But you're right, having a positive frame of mind will certainly help. Everything I've read so far about cancer says the same."

"And not to feel guilty or that you've failed if it comes back or gets worse before it gets better."

"Be open to letting the light heal me."

"Exactly."

"I've been thinking a lot about Will lately. Not your Will, but Austin's brother."

Libby stopped the cup halfway to her mouth and asked for clarification.

"I wish I could make amends with him too."

"Whatever for? Did you meet him?"

"Yes. Briefly. Austin was so upset that he'd enlisted in the Navy. Thought he'd thrown his life away. He wanted him to go to college. He had a scholarship, I think, down here at one of the schools, for football or baseball. I don't remember which. But no one could talk him out of serving. His parents tried. Everyone did. Before he deployed, we all had a terrible argument. I always felt bad about that."

"You three or just you?"

"All three of us. Actually, I should correct myself. Austin and I were the ones arguing. Will was fine about the whole thing. He didn't hold any resentment. Austin's the same way. Very trusting. I think that's what made him so angry. He told him he'd believed some recruiter's B.S. about noble service. And who knew? You wound up falling in love and marrying a Navy SEAL just like Will. It was through Coop that we got to understand the whole brotherhood thing. I would like to tell Will that now I get it."

Libby could imagine the conversations they'd had. It didn't take much to feel what it would be like to have both her parents against something and try to stop her. She pictured her uncle sitting very calmly in a chair, listening to them with a smile on his face, just like how Coop would be. Hearing them but not agreeing with them. Coop's family had taken his enlistment with a sense of pride, as so many of the farmers' boys went into one or another branch of the service before coming home to work on the family farm. And although she didn't know for sure, she chose the version she liked best: He understood where they were coming from and loved them anyway, because it was his commitment, his path he was following and not theirs.

She thought about Karen. *Is a new story starting there?* she wondered. Perhaps there would be a way to mend broken fences thirty years later. Who knew?

"Did he act like Dad?" she finally asked.

"Couldn't tell them apart. Will stole a kiss from me when I thought he was Austin. Austin was furious. I think he was a little mad at me, too, for not knowing I was kissing his brother."

"That's funny, Mom."

"You know how your dad walks, with that long gait? He walks like a ballet dancer, very graceful, in a masculine way."

"Like Coop too."

"Yes, that's it. He danced at our wedding and was very popular with all my friends. The ladies loved him."

Libby began to wonder if her mother suspected anything about Karen or had overheard a conversation mentioning her. She couldn't remember having much of a conversation at all about Uncle Will all her years growing up.

If it was meant to be, it will be.

Her mother was ready to take a morning nap, so she helped Ynez walk her to the elevator and up to the second floor. Then they tucked her in her giant bed. She brought a glass of water and set it on the bedside table while Ynez handed her mother the pills she was supposed to take mid-morning.

"I do get tired easier. I notice that since the surgery," her mother said after taking swallows and setting the glass down.

Libby fluffed up the pillow beneath her head. "You just rest. Why don't you have sweet dreams about telling Will all those nice things? I'm sure he'd like to hear them," Libby whispered.

She began to straighten up when her mother clutched her hand. "Thank you."

"For what?"

"For putting up with me. For helping Austin out, helping

me out, and for your friendship. I'm not always easy on you, and I'm sorry about that. I want you to know I regret that sometimes."

"Nothing more needs to be said. I'm grateful for you, too, Mom. And I mean it when I talked about having that conversation with Will."

Her mother released her hand and lay back with a smile, closing her eyes. Her face was peaceful and without strain. The way she lay so still, it gave Libby a fright, as if she was seeing into the future.

That image haunted her all the way home, until she got the call from Christy that Cooper would be coming home tomorrow morning.

"How did it go?"

"I gather it was a success. They made some rescues, about ten girls, from what Kyle says. No one is coming home injured."

"Thanks for letting me know. He's got his truck at the base, so I'll wait for him at home. How are things at the Lansdowne household?"

"You heard our news?"

"What news?"

"We're expecting again. Quite a surprise. Not sure where we'll put everyone. Kyle might have to bunk up in the garage."

"You let me know if I can help out in any way."

"You have your hands full. How's your mom?"

"She just came home from the hospital yesterday, got a good night's sleep she says. She looks good, but we're not out of the woods yet. Still exploring the options. But she feels better and is at home, and that's all that counts right now."

"That's right. Well, give her my love, then."

She stopped by the store and purchased some of Coop's favorite things: strawberries and whipped cream, for their first welcome home night together. It was part of their routine, to celebrate the good times and the rest would take care of themselves.

CHAPTER 15

DUE TO THE raid and the number of casualties, the Team was moved quickly from the motel to another one in a neighboring town, Todos Santos, where it was thought their profiles could fade into the tourist community. So, instead of returning to their old base, a private contractor team quietly removed any additional evidence the SEALs were ever in residence there and brought any equipment or articles left behind to their new location. It was thought too dangerous for Kyle and his men to ever return there.

The long drive in the middle of the night with the shivering and scared girls was an experience Coop would never forget. So traumatized by what had befallen them, the girls were forced to ride in a van with ten new strange men, and although they were the rescue team, it only prolonged what was a harrowing few days for them. Some of them had been beaten, others were hungry and dehydrated, and then there were a handful that had been forced into sex.

It was something Coop thought he might bring up later. As medics, they were trained to treat injuries of the physical kind but were not trained counselors, other than treating men and women in combat situations. Clearly, a case could be made for future SEAL medics to be trained in psychological warfare, treatment of the abused and traumatized. He felt so inadequate dishing out waters, blankets, granola bars, and pain meds. He checked small cuts and bruises but couldn't give them what they really needed, the counseling to help alleviate their suffering. So, in this way, he felt he was only prolonging the mental injury.

One of the girls who had been raped had begun to scream and cry uncontrollably and had to be sedated. Of course, she had to be held down to deliver the injection, which didn't help the situation any. The edge in the room and the unspoken trauma of the other girls hung in the ceiling of the bus like a damp, lethal fog. For many, a bus ride brought on remembrances of summer camps and church trips or, for some of the guys, transport in foreign countries, like their trip across the desert in Morocco or fleeing from the raiding parties in Nigeria through red farmland. For the girls, their most recent trip in a school bus was the journey from freedom to bondage and an uncertain future.

The one thing they needed was human touch and kind words. The men did what they could to settle fears and offer smiles and encouragement that they were indeed in good company, but many of the girls didn't trust anything coming from the men and were just holding on with all the strength they had left. There were no smiles. They'd seen too much. None of their lives had ever prepared them for the several days of hell they'd experienced.

Coop was sad that he couldn't do more.

A team of U.S. doctors and social workers were meeting them at the new destination and would assist in recording the abuses, obtaining names and accounts of the events, allow access to their families and arrange their transportation back home. The school they came from was just North of San Diego, but the girls were from all over the United States.

He tried to encourage the three girls sitting in front of him that they could spread out, but they chose to stay huddled together. Not one of the three made eye contact with him. It nearly brought him to tears to think of his daughter perhaps someday doing something with her friends and winding up in a situation like this. He regretted not being able to kill the tangos more than they did.

To make matters worse, Kyle would come under fire for having used the level of violence they used. Although he didn't talk about it, he knew his LPO chose to drive for that very reason, so he could be by himself to think about his future on the Teams.

Now that he was going to have his fourth child.

What would he do if they told him his career was over?

It was the one thing Coop didn't care for about the military. Even a good outcome could cause international ripples and, in the end, be classified a failure. He hoped that wasn't the case here. It all depended on who was going to step in and negotiate on their behalf and who was on the receiving end from the Mexican government.

There were so many players—players who negotiated in good faith and those who didn't. Some from the State Department didn't know the first thing about real combat, the real face of war. It was all theory to them. They devised some of the crazy plans the SEALs were charged with carrying out without the knowledge or consultation of someone who had been on the ground and knew the odds of success. Somehow, they were supposed to do the best they could with the information they were given.

He prayed this would be the case.

Coop knew every man on the bus tonight understood what was at risk of happening. None of the men were injured, and they'd gotten out all the girls they found, but there were probably thousands packed in vans and trains and shipping containers being trafficked all over the world, feeling all alone, worrying and wondering if anyone would ever come to rescue them and make their nightmare end. And there would be the officials in Mexico who would feel the SEALs overstepped their permission and would want someone to pay. There could have been civilians injured or killed tonight. It all depended on who they were.

Now was the time when everyone would have their doubts, because they were trained to execute, not hesitate and think about what they were doing. It wasn't fair, but they could be judged by this. It could be the reason any of them were kicked out of the Teams, along with their leader. He imagined Kyle calculated all this while he was driving, so he could report how many killed and what had been damaged, blown up, broken into, or injured. He feared for the life of the cook and her two helpers they were not authorized to extract.

So much was at stake. It was dark. He'd be up all night. And then he'd have to write a report and talk to teams of State

Department staff and someone from the Navy. After all that was done, signed, shaking of hands finished, and waving goodbye over, then and only then would he be able to shower and fall into bed for a few hours. In the early evening, they were told they'd be on their way back to Coronado and their loved ones.

Kyle didn't have to mention that any number of the personnel he had to meet with could render a verdict that he'd acted inappropriately. That could delay the return home. Flags might be added to his file. Some might get written up and given leave.

This last gauntlet was what he hated about the military.

But there just wasn't any way around it.

As dawn broke over the horizon, they came to the outskirts of the artist community. The town itself was still asleep. Shopkeepers hosed down the sidewalks in front of their stores. Food and beverages were delivered in covered trucks. Teams of service help and tour guides reported for work. The people behind the village of shops and entertainment, the ones who helped keep the wheels of commerce turning profitably, were reporting for duty on this bright morning, totally oblivious of all the danger around them and that some girls had been rescued from a cartel that had the gall to profit off human flesh. Men and women who would steal away a young girl's future for a few dollars of profit.

Kyle spoke into his cell, getting directions. Coop walked down the aisle to see if he could assist him.

"And then how far out is it?"

Coop heard the squawk but not the words of the response.

"You want me to hold the phone. Are they giving you any GPS help, Kyle?" Coop asked his LPO.

Kyle handed him the phone. "Have them explain it to you. Maybe my ears are all shot. I'm not getting anywhere, and I sure as hell don't want a police escort."

"Roger that. Yo, this is Special Operator Cal—"

"Don't give them all that. You're a Navy Medic, son," Kyle interrupted him.

"U.S. Navy Medic Cooper here. Can you give me coordinates or an address I can do a map on?"

"I can send a link."

Kyle was shaking his head no.

"I'm afraid we're about out of power. Address please?" Coop asked. He was rewarded when Kyle nodded his approval.

Coop had to ask the heavily-accented man three times to spell the name of the street and then hung up before any other questions arose. "Who was that?"

"Our State liaison here. Obviously, he's not done this before."

"You gotta wonder, sometimes."

"Can you call Collins?"

"You have him on speed dial?"

"Go into my address book. I have it under just C."

Coop found it and dialed. He heard a double click as the call went through an international line and then hit an answering voice, but then Collins picked up, coughing.

"Kyle, you guys made it to Santos?"

"Kyle's driving the bus, sir. This is Cooper. I got an address but no directions. We're on a little highway—" He bent down to look outside for a marker.

"Highway 6," Kyle said.

"Highway 6, heading toward Todos Santos. It says five kilometers away from the City Center."

"Okay, let me pull it up. Your liaison didn't give you directions?"

"We didn't want to take the link, sir. But if you could."

"Yeah, coming your way." Coop waited a few seconds and then got the beep as the link to the map came through.

"Got it. We'll call you when we arrive, okay?"

"Let me speak to Kyle, will you?"

Cooper handed the phone over. Whatever was said remained a mystery. Kyle verbally agreed, answering, 'Understood,' and then hung up the phone.

"Press that thing, and let's get the map on here," Kyle instructed him.

A map appeared and tracked the phone location and a route to the motel they were heading to. In about twenty minutes, they arrived at the metal gates encircling a modest cluster of bungalows surrounding a courtyard. "Hotel Luna" flashed on the blue neon sign.

Coop noticed four large black SUVs parked inside the fencing with diplomatic plates. A tall gentleman in a blue blazer opened the gate to allow them entry. As they passed by him, Coop spotted his white earpiece.

Kyle leaned over the steering wheel for a second as if praying they'd arrived, finally. Then he got up, gave Coop a smirk, and made his announcement.

"Okay, we're here. Ladies, we're going to let you get off the bus first so you can meet with the staff here who are going to help you get fresh clothes and a shower. They're going to ask some questions, allow you to phone home, and then get you safely on your way."

A couple of the girls clapped their hands but stopped when it didn't catch fire. Solemnly, they moved down the aisle, shuffling their feet. Some made eye contact and whispered soft "thank you"s to the men. Others kept their eyes fixed on the ground. T.J. brought the girl who had been sedated, holding her carefully. Her arm limply swung by her side; her head slumped into his chest. He maneuvered down the steps and gave her over to two men dressed in blue scrubs who placed her on a stretcher and strapped her to the bed.

Kyle waited for the girls to be absorbed by the personnel on the ground. Then he closed the door to the outside, asked T.J. to take his seat, and looked at his little squad.

"I'm going to lay it out to you straight, from what I've been told. We're going to have to answer for the deaths of several Mexican citizens and possibly a couple of civilians. We don't know what the survivors are going to say, but I'm fairly confident they'll portray us as conquering heroes."

He looked down and added, "But the Navy may see it differently. Our job was only to get Rufus. Then they amended the orders to allow us to rescue the girls. Everything we did tonight achieved that goal, but every action by every one of you is going to be called into question. Why am I telling you this? I want you all to tell the truth. All of it. Don't worry about how it will sound. Just tell the truth. Don't try to make it into a story that you think they want to hear. They're looking for blame or, perhaps, some kind of ill intent. You just tell them where you came from and why you did what you did. And for most of you, you acted on my orders. If anyone is to be punished for this event tonight, it should be me, because you were just following my direction."

He scanned the tired crew sitting to rapt attention in front of him. "Don't worry about me. I signed on to this. Don't be afraid of their questions or the pointedness you think they bring with them. It might take hours, or it could be over quickly. But the truth is our best bet, what will save us. The consistency with our answers is what we need here. No comparing notes, just tell the goddamned truth!"

Coop heard scattered mumbling and a few choice swear words.

"I've been through these debriefings before, more times than I've liked, but I want you to know I'm extremely proud of each and every one of you who acted bravely and put your own lives on the line to help protect these girls and your fellow brothers. It's been an honor to conduct this raid with you and to serve as your leader. But don't worry about me. Whatever happens, I'll be fine."

Armando raised his hand. Kyle nodded to him.

"Where's this coming from?"

Coop could see a couple of Navy regulars and two men in suits forming a delegation, headed straight for the bus.

"I got a head's up from Collins who said there's a particular Naval officer upset with the loss of life for those Mexican citizens. Apparently, an undercover CIA operative is missing, as well as a U.S. citizen."

CHAPTER 16

LIBBY WAS MAKING dinner when Cooper called.

"Getting on a plane tonight. I'll be late."

"OMG. Christy said tomorrow morning! That's wonderful news." She turned to the kids. "Daddy's coming home tonight."

A collective cheer went up. Gillian was setting the table. Will had just turned off the television on orders from Libby.

"Yeah, well, it could have easily been in the morning. We had a whole day of debriefing. Kyle probably told her that so she wouldn't worry if we got delayed. It was the most grueling questioning I've ever had. They nitpicked everything. I don't want to talk about it anymore. Oh, and Jameson re-upped for another four years for a bonus."

"Oh, that's good for them with the baby and all."

"Yeah." He paused. "Just know that I love you, and I'll try not to wake you up. It will be after midnight. I just got a shower and a little nap, but I'm beat."

"Sorry. You better wake me up, Coop."

He sighed on the phone. "Well, all right. If you insist."

The pause on his end made her nervous until she heard the

low, rumbling chuckle that made her knees wobble.

After dinner, she put the kids to bed early, straightened up the kitchen, and changed the sheets on her bed. Then she took a shower and splashed some lavender body oil on her back, her chest, and her legs before she crawled into bed.

She awoke to the feel of his kisses on her neck. He'd spooned behind her quietly and, like he said, didn't wake her up. He smelled like an old airport—faint hint of cigarettes, cheap perfume, and too many people.

His hands cupped her breasts as she rolled back against him. One hand smoothed over her front then down to her belly until his fingers found her pulsing sex and tried to satisfy her. But it was no use. Even two fingers weren't nearly enough as she writhed next to him, listening to his heavy breathing and the soft moan of a man in just as much need as she was.

He was quick to let her feel his hardness in the cleft between her cheeks. She pulled one knee toward her chest, and he positioned his hip to allow his slow thrust to fully engulf her, rooting deep and urgently demanding full access. He strained against himself, trying not to come. When she touched their union and then ringed the base of his shaft with her fingers and squeezed his balls, he pushed her over on her belly and pumped furiously, splitting her knees farther apart and gripping her hips to hold her up against him.

In the quiet of the bedroom, with the sounds of the ocean cavorting with the beach somewhere in the distance, she felt the jolt of his spilling and she released, joining him in that place where they always went, loving the passion and unable to get enough even at the peak of perfect orgasm. He held her until she stopped shaking, kissing her neck, massaging her belly, and pressing her bud with his forefinger.

Nobody could play her body like he could. In the tangle of lavender-scented sheets, his stubbled cheeks against hers, his lips whispering things she could dream about for decades, she brought him home in every way she could, because he was her rock, her private kind of elixir of maleness which ignited all the female spirits within her belly. She cried out for him and felt the hot tears streaming down her cheeks at the realization that life was so very fragile and fleeting, and she was the luckiest woman alive to have such a man share her bed.

"Missed you so much, Libby," he whispered at last.

"Missed you, Coop. Welcome home, sweetheart."

"Nothing better," he said, kissing all the way down her spine and then back up to her ear. One large hand gripped her jaw, turning her head enough to kiss the corner of her lips. She pressed her backside into him, still locked deep inside her, and begged for him to stay there.

SHE AWOKE ALONE, awakened by the sounds of the kids screaming and running around the house with Cooper chasing both of them. She threw on a robe and made it out to the bacon and coffee smells in the kitchen.

Cooper wore one of Will's capes, the ones Libby had made for him when he was into dressing up as superheroes a whole two years ago, when he was a baby, it seemed. Now at nine, he was way too old for such things, but that didn't apply to his dad, who growled and pounced and ran, the red cape flapping in the morning sunlight, revealing his red, white, and blue boxers and his hairy legs.

Gillian was still in her princess nightgown, Will in his penguin flannel pajamas he got for Christmas.

Will took out his wooden sword and slay the evil creature with the red cape, who fell to the ground, bony legs bicycling up to the ceiling as he did a death rattle. His arms flailed to the sides and then went limp as he died.

Gillian pounced on his belly after he was dead, and Libby heard the huge "umph" from Cooper as she landed hard.

"We got you, evil dragon," she yelled. "Ha-ha! He's dead!"

"But wait. He's coming alive!" Coop said as his fingers found Gillian's waist and he tickled her until she fell off.

"Stop it, dragon. I command you!" Will said, pointing his sword at Coop's face. "Or I shall chop your head off and you cannot rise again!"

Cooper was done for, arms crashing to the sides, legs clawing against the floor, and then was perfectly still.

Libby lifted Gillian off her dad and came to Coop's rescue. "Come on, you two. Daddy's been working hard, and it's time to give him a break." She knelt beside him as he opened his eyes and then encircled her in his arms, hugging her close to him.

"Now I have the great prize. The Queen of San Diego!" he said, kissing her neck.

She laughed against his chest with his arms still around her. The bow at his neck from the cap had come undone as she rested her head against him and reveled in his heavy breathing.

"Oh boy. I don't have to go in for a workout this morning.

You two play hard. I'm having a hard time keeping up with you," Coop said as he sat then stood and helped Libby up. He gave her a proper squeeze and kiss before he slapped her on the rear and let her go. "Coffee, woman. I demand coffee."

"Your wish is my command," she said back to him and slipped away.

"Yuck," said Will under his breath, and he and Gillian took their places at the breakfast table.

Libby poured them both coffee with half-and-half while Coop dished up bacon, eggs, and popped two pieces of toast into the toaster.

She hadn't noticed it at first, but the tie on her robe had slipped, leaving a big gaping opening, showing off much of her breast and tummy. The kids hadn't noticed, but Coop did, slipping an arm around her waist and pressing her against his bare chest. "Vera, vera nice."

She had to work not to spill her coffee on his back. She kissed him back.

"Your mom called this morning and asked if we could drop by after the kids go to school," he said.

"I didn't hear a thing. I guess I needed the rest," Libby said in response.

"When can we see Grandma?" asked Gillian.

"You know what? We'll ask her today, kiddo," answered Libby.

"So if she doesn't have boobs anymore, does that mean she can't breast feed?" asked Will.

"Did you tell him that?" asked Cooper.

"I'm not sure where he got that from. Who told you, Will?"

"Gillian told me if you take a woman's breasts away, she can't nurse her baby, and the baby will die."

The comment surprised Libby, but Gillian blushed, denying she'd ever said anything of the kind to her brother.

"Fact is, she's beyond the age of having babies, but yes, if she wasn't, then the baby would have to drink out of a bottle because that's what they're for," Libby instructed them both.

Cooper wiggled his eyebrows up and down. "And they're wonderful for kissing, too. I like to grab them and touch them like—" He reached for her, and she jumped out of the way but, this time, did spill her coffee. Both the kids laughed.

While Cooper took them to school, Libby straightened the bed and cleaned up the kitchen. She was in the shower when he returned and joined her.

"Do you have to go into the Team building today?" she asked as he soaped off her backside.

"Nope. We're off for a week, unless called in for more questions."

"Oh right, you started telling me about that. How come the inquiry?"

"That," he said as he turned her towards him and began soaping off her front side, "is on a need-to-know basis. It's top secret and totally classified. You'd have to torture me for a week to get it out of me."

"Uh huh," Libby answered, washing soap from his chest with the shower wand. She handed him the device, stepped out onto a bathmat, and began to dry off. "So you want to go over to Mom and Dad's then?"

She handed a towel to Cooper. "Sure. Your dad said he'd

be home until noon, so let's go over first thing."

THEY DROVE OVER in Libby's SUV and parked on the street, which was deserted today. At the doorway, they met Benjamin, who was the Fijian nurse who looked after Carla in the early morning hours until after breakfast. He was a huge man with intricate tattoos on his forearms, his hands as big as plates, perhaps even bigger than Cooper's. His handshake was warm, very firm, yet gentle, Libby thought.

"Your mamma is quite a lady, Miss Libby. And they were right about her being stubborn. Wow. That's all I can say." He grinned to both of them.

"Nice to meet you, Benjamin," Coop said as he shook the nurse's hand. "How was her night?"

"She's doing much better today, and I don't think she's in as much pain. Ynez knows about the medications she's taking, but last night, I actually got to sleep some, so that was good." He grinned again, his perfect white teeth shining in the light of the doorway.

"Thank you so much. Do you guys need anything at all?" asked Libby.

"Not a thing. Your dad's been very good to us."

They watched him waddle down the walkway to his car.

"Kids, come on inside," came Carla's voice from the kitchen.

She was in a pretty pink robe and matching fuzzy slippers, having her cup of coffee.

"See what Austin bought me?" She wiggled her toes showing off the slippers and pointing to the robe.

Ynez handed Libby a mug of coffee and then went to get one for Cooper. "I have to talk to him about those things. Leaving feathers all over the house," Ynez sputtered. "I'm going to be chasing those things all summer long, you watch."

"They're pretty. Impractical but very pretty."

"I'm not wearing them outside. I've got my outdoor slippers for that," said Carla. "I've always wanted little pompoms on my feet ever since I can remember."

Dr. Brownlee entered the kitchen, greeted Coop, and then gave a kiss on Libby's cheek. "I see you're back in good shape. How was the mission?"

"You're not supposed to ask, Dad. It's top secret, need-to-know," Libby corrected him.

"I know, but—"

"Mexico. I can tell you that. We were tracking some human smugglers, which have exploded on the scene lately. I'm sure you've been reading all about it."

"Terrible situation. I hope we're able to get a handle on it all."

"Well, we scored one for the good guys, and that's probably all I can say," answered Coop.

"I'm not surprised. I would never doubt you, Cooper. So does that mean you won't have to go over so soon again?"

"No, ma'am. Doesn't mean anything of the sort. It's the luck of the draw. We're on right now, so if something comes up, and I know they're working on stuff all the time, we'll be tasked. But when, who knows? We aren't even sure where."

"Kind of makes it hard to plan family things, outings, or vacations," said Dr. Brownlee.

"You remember our regular deployment schedules when I first met you guys. I long for those days—four months work-up, four months overseas, four months home and recovery. But we miss stuff all the time. I was lucky to be home for both Gillian and Will's births. Some men don't get that."

The doorbell rang, and Ynez scurried to go answer it. She returned and said, "There is that lady at the door again, Libby. She's asking for Dr. Brownlee."

Libby looked at Cooper who looked at Dr. Brownlee who looked at his wife.

"What young lady?" asked Carla.

"Well, let's meet her. Do you suppose we should let her in?" he asked Cooper.

"Let me go get her." Coop left the room.

"Who is this person, Austin?"

"I'll let her explain," he said, walking over to his wife and placing his hand on her shoulder.

Coop and Karen Watson entered the kitchen. Karen's eyes got huge when she spotted Dr. Brownlee.

"You're uncle Austin. Oh my God! You look just like the pictures!" She came over and shook his hand.

Carla's jaw had dropped, her eyes round, her body frozen in place with her coffee mug halfway to her mouth.

"This is my wife, Carla. Carla Brownlee."

"Nice to meet you, Carla," Karen said.

Libby's stomach began to churn at how informal she was her mother, not calling her "Mrs. Brownlee."

Once again, Karen was dressed in running pants, this time bright orange and black stripes with orange-colored running shoes. She wore a lightweight windbreaker with a center zipper pocket. She slipped her car keys inside and zipped it up discretely. She didn't have a purse.

"You want coffee?" Ynez asked her.

"Sure. Black please." She walked over to Libby and shook her hand again and gave Coop a hug like she had before. Her attitude was goofy, kind of self-conscious.

"That was awkward. I should have hugged you, Libby, my cousin. Coop, you would be my cousin by marriage, right?" She accepted the mug of coffee and took a sip.

"Right," Libby said.

"So young lady—Karen, is it?" Carla leaned forward and asked, "Just how do you come to think we are relatives of yours? Who told you this?"

"Yes, ma'am." She stood in front of a loveseat directly across the little room from Carla and Dr. Brownlee. "May I?" she asked.

"Of course, please sit."

Karen got comfortable, took another sip of coffee, and began. "Will Brownlee is my father. He never knew that I was on the way. He and my mother dated casually for a few weeks before he deployed to Grenada. On the day she found out she was pregnant came word that Will had been killed on the mission there."

She continued, "Mom knew his family was already dealing with a lot, so she decided to move back to Oregon where her folks lived at the time and intended on coming back to San Diego and introducing me." Her lip turned down, and her shoulders slumped. "After I was born, Mom reconsidered that and decided to raise me on her own. I never knew I had a father until recently. I mean—I knew I had a father and that he had died, but I didn't know about all of you. I asked about him ever since I was little, and she wouldn't tell me anything. So I took a DNA test, and there was a match. It gave me your name, Dr. Brownlee, as being nearly an exact match. I think that's the way it goes with twins. When I told her I was coming down for the San Diego marathon and I was going to try to find my father and that he might be alive, that's when she told me my father was your twin."

"Did you know anything about this, Austin?" Carla asked.

"No, only what Libby told me. They met here at the house a couple of days ago, when you were in the hospital. I found out when I got home."

"Did Will ever mention her mother to you?" asked Carla.

"Not that I recall. If you will remember, we weren't too keen on his joining up. Those were dark days."

"I do," Carla said to her coffee mug. "Is your mother still alive?" she asked Karen.

"Oh, she is. She's coming down for the marathon to cheer me on." Karen dropped the bombshell like she was decorating cookies. "I haven't told her that I found you people yet."

Cooper and Libby sat in two chairs facing the conversation area. Karen couldn't keep her eyes off Cooper and Dr. Brownlee, as she kept focusing her attention from one man to the other, back and forth.

Libby felt like she and her mom weren't even in the room.

"Isn't it a miracle? I go from having no family to suddenly having all of you?"

Libby's heart fell through the floor when she saw the pained expression on her mother's face. She had been right.

The news wasn't exactly what her mom wanted to hear. Even her slippers wilted.

CHAPTER 17

COOPER WAS SUMMONED by Kyle to a select meeting of just a handful of Team 3 stalwarts, mostly men who had been with him the longest. They chose the back room at the Scupper.

"Heard about your mom, Coop. It must be a scarry time for Libby," whispered Armando. "Sorry if I wasn't supposed to hear, but old gaff-master here," he pointed to Kyle, "couldn't keep his mouth shut."

Kyle hung his head. "Guilty as charged. Sorry, Coop."

"Not really a problem. I was just giving Libby some time to settle with it. But I think she's started telling a few people now."

"What's the prognosis?" Armando asked.

Coop angled his head, not sure how to respond. "We're still learning stuff. Nobody's making promises to her. Of course, she thinks she can grow her own vegetables and juice herself healthy. But then, that's Carla."

Fredo and Kyle chuckled. "I'm surprised you haven't given her your tofu lecture, Coop. Man, did that piss me off when you came at me with all that shit."

"It worked. You have offspring to prove it," Coop reminded him.

"Yeah, thanks to you, we got a full house. Mia still wants more. I'm making sure I'm getting a steady diet of junk food, sort of my male contraceptive device, now that we know that stuff is reversible. But I never would have believed it."

Coop smiled at his quirky friend.

T.J. Talbot sauntered in, late. "Sorry, Kyle. Had some issues at home that couldn't be helped."

"No problem," Kyle nodded. "We were just talking about male contraception."

Everyone laughed.

Coop made the proper explanation. "Not really, T.J., but we were talking about Fredo's—"

"Yeah, I know all about it, Coop. Thanks. Fredo, I still think it was all in your head. No way eating health food could change your sperm count. Or you have funny-looking sperm that look dead in a petri dish. Something like that shit. But no way some fuckin' bean curd would get my wife pregnant. I *know* how it works!"

Coop slapped him on the back. "That's okay. When I'm running marathons in my nineties, I won't remind you. But I'll wave as I pass your wheelchair."

"You just try. By then, I'll have a rocket-powered chair and bionic legs and arms. Except for a few nodes and plugs and wires and shit, I'll look like a thirty-year-old version of myself, and I'll smoke your bony ass. My legs won't have varicose veins, and my dick will be bigger than it is today."

The challenge was on. Coop quietly set down his mineral

water with lime, took a tomato from his omelet, placed it on his fork, and threw it at T.J.'s front, where it splattered all over his navy-blue tee shirt. "Yeah, and your legs will be plastic, then. But you go ahead with that vision." He looked around the table. "Anyone want to take bets?"

Most everyone laughed. Coop noticed Armando was a little silent this morning, but he left that unattended.

"Speaking of marathons, anyone doing the San Diego?" asked Fredo.

Armando shook his head. T.J. shrugged. "Some of the guys were talking about it on the flight home. You should talk to Jake, Jason, those guys. I think they're up to it. How about you, Coop? You love those."

"Hadn't considered it this year." With the discussion ended, he added, "So why are we here, Kyle?"

"Thank God," breathed Kyle. "I was beginning to worry I'd chosen the wrong friends for this little pow-wow." He folded his hands on the table and made eye contact with each man, one by one, and then began.

"They might toss me, gents."

"No fuckin' way," spat T.J.

"It could happen. I'm waiting on a review that went up the ladder for a signoff. I do have friends in high places, but not sure they're in the right branch of the tree, so to speak."

Coop knew this was coming, but he didn't say so.

"I assume you're getting this from Collins?" Armando asked.

Their liaison, who wore a Trident, was delegated to desk duty because of a mistake he'd made in deployment. It was a

SEAL's billet but not one that many would take. He wasn't of the same stature as their former liaison, Master Chief Timmons, who had retired, but it was his job to look after Kyle's platoon. Cooper was starting not to like the man, concerned he might be the weakest link in the chain of command.

"I am."

T.J. was careful. "I'm not sure all that's accurate. Have you read the report, Kyle?"

"No."

"Fuck that. Timmons would let me read anything going into my file," huffed Fredo.

"Look, that's not why I called you in here. I know you have my back, just as I have yours. But I want your honest opinion. Do you think it's time?"

Coop could see he was emotional about even saying it. The group was aghast.

"You mean you're gonna quit?" T.J. barked. He was getting frostier by the second.

"We don't quit, Kyle," reminded Armando. "We stay to the end. We do whatever it takes, but we don't quit until we are done. You gotta ask yourself if you still want to fight. That's the real question and not one any of us can answer for you."

As usual, Armando's eloquent manner, coming from the quiet side of their ethos, said it perfectly. Coop recognized the beauty of how he was able to scale it right down to the size it should be to tackle the problem. And it was Kyle's problem. But like everything they did, it also affected the Team. Kyle was such an integral portion of the Team's success, not having his leadership would domino over many of the men. He wasn't sure there wouldn't be a wholesale quit. The turmoil would continue, too, if Collins had any say in their replacement.

"You mentioned that someone was upset with the results of our mission to Baja. But do you have any details? Any facts to back that up?" asked Coop.

"Not specifically, except that we killed four people, three of whom were Mexican and one person of questionable nationality, possibly American or perhaps dual citizenship, who was employed by the CIA."

"So they had a mess to clean up," added Fredo. "Someone lost some money too. You know that factors in this. Someone paid to bring those girls in and auction them off. Someone has to either return the money or pay the consequences. Someone's dirty, Kyle. That's not you or even what we did."

"Could be." Kyle did appear worried. "I've been trying to think about what we could have done differently. Frankly, I'm all out of options, and not having all the facts is more than a little stressful. I mean, I don't know if I should get an attorney, start sprucing up my resume, or put my head on straight for the next engagement. They want Rufus. That was what they really wanted."

"And someone, when confronted with the fact that all of us witnessed the girls held there, knew we could save them and that turning our backs on them would cause some heads to roll. But yes, clearly someone got to Rufus and perhaps warned him," added Coop. He saw a big spiderweb, shadowy creatures and so many secrets it was clear someone was going to take the fall.

"And Collins might not be the cause here, but I'll bet he's close to someone who is," said T.J. "I'll bet he knows more than he's letting out."

"Oh, for sure. I get that, T.J.," answered Kyle. "I just don't know what I should be doing."

Armando weighed in. "I think we gotta get vocal. Maybe we need someone's help on the outside. What about Colin Riley?"

"We've met him, but Tucker is closest to him. I'll bet he could help," said Coop. "You want me to ask Tucker to get in touch?"

"I got his number too," said Kyle. "He's kind of rogue, though. I just don't want to have him interfere if there isn't a problem. That could get me tossed as well."

"Look, Kyle, you've *already got a problem.* This has all the earmarks of a major blown cover plan, a big issue, not only for you but all of us. If this is a whitewash, then we're going to be asked to lie or change our stories or tell on each other." Fredo crossed his arms. "And I'm not going to do it."

"Nor am I," said Armando.

"Me neither, Boss," added T.J.

"I'm not gonna start lying now, Kyle. I got too much respect for our Team, for you, and for all the guys we lost doing good things. I think about the betrayal of the Secretary of State—that could have sourced somewhere deep inside the State Department or one of the intelligence branches—who knows? It was never talked about because the public wasn't told the truth. We're kind of used to that, aren't we?" Coop felt better saying his peace. "I think Armando's right. We get vocal. But I think Riley will know the right buttons to push."

Armando added another gem. "Kyle, no offense, but you're too close to it, and that's the way it should be. I think Riley needs to be contacted by one of us, because we're worried you're being railroaded. If it goes south, one of us can take the heat for it, not make it worse for you. You're already committed, up to your neck."

Everyone else agreed.

Coop jumped in. "I think you can trust Tucker. Now I wish Sven hadn't been held up with Kelly." Then Coop had another idea. "Unless that was the plan. Kelly would have sniffed out who had a hand in this. But she wasn't there."

"You think the ambassador made up a fake mission, a ruse to keep her away?" asked Kyle.

"We should ask her," Coop answered. "Let me talk to Tucker and to Kelly. One of you go with. We'll have that little talk and see if she's back yet, and then we'll have Tucker and Kelly request assistance from Riley. It won't take longer than a couple of days. Unless that's too long?"

"I'm just sitting here."

T.J. spoke up. "I'll go with you on that meet and greet, Coop. Unless someone else wants in?"

"You go ahead. We got things at home going on," said Armando.

Fredo shook his head.

Armando's comment caught Coop's attention, but again, he kept it to himself.

"Okay, gents. If something comes along, I'll give you a heads-up. But I appreciate this. If anything gets too hot, you let me know. You save yourself, okay?"

"Will do. And, Kyle, go take the kids and Christy out somewhere." Coop saw the smirk develop on Kyle's face.

"She's not exactly hungry these days."

"So it's true. Your little team is covering all the bases now, including home plate?" chuckled Fredo.

"Looks that way, if it all goes well. And she doesn't know about any of this. I want it kept that way."

Coop vowed to support this man, no matter what. He knew the rest of his brothers felt the same way. He'd been there for all of them for years. He was an exceptional leader, a rare talent, and not at all expendable. Coop's anger was getting routed to Collins, and he recognized that was a dangerous thing to let slip. He'd have to be careful with that. But he'd put a bug into Tucker's ear about how he felt.

CHAPTER 18

WILL'S SOCCER TOURNAMENT was on the agenda this weekend. Libby had signed up to organize the snack bar, which was a fundraiser for the club. Coop had shopped her list and brought the chips, hot dogs, sodas, candy, and fruit for smoothies, dropping them off ahead of her. He promised to be back for Will's game.

The little plywood shed had not been cleaned properly by the previous parent manning the booth, so after she placed all the cold drinks and fruit into the refrigerator, she ran a tub of hot soapy water, wiped down everything, swept the floor, and scoured the painted wooden counter. With a fresh coat of paint and some things added to the kitchen, like a new larger blender for the smoothies, some used lightweight patio furniture, and a couple of old umbrellas, she could make the stand more attractive and sell more items for the club. She put it on her list to see if she could get a small budget, so it didn't have to come out of her own wallet.

"Hi there. Do you need some help?"

Libby had been straightening the cups and paper plates beneath the counter. When she stood up, Karen's smiling face was perfectly framed in the opening.

"Oh, hi. I wasn't expecting you to come today."

"I know that." She shrugged. "But I'm here. Thought I'd watch Will play. I knew my uncle said he'd be at the game, so I thought I would, you know, just try to plug in."

Her mother would have a much better word for it. She hated herself for mistrusting the woman so, but she had no real way of assessing if she was actually the same kind of person she was presenting. Her mother didn't like her, Libby knew that already. Carla often had the best instincts of any of the rest of the family combined.

But Libby found it hard to turn her down. "Sure. They have another half hour of warmup. I was going to get some hot dogs on the portable griller. You want to do that? Then we can stack the buns beside it and set up the paper plates and napkins for when it's lunchtime."

"Be glad to." She stood next to Libby, washing her hands thoroughly in the stainless-steel tub. "You have any more liquid soap?"

"Oh, darn, I forgot. I think I have a couple bars here—" Libby scrounged under the sink cabinet and found a package of lavender-scented soap bars. "Voila!"

"Give me one of those. They smell divine."

"Somebody was using their head, it seems."

"The hot dogs are in the fridge?"

"Yes, ma'am. And I've already plugged the griller in and sprayed the rollers."

She ripped open the package and looked for the trash can.

"Oops, didn't start one. You can grab one of those big

black bags for now. We'll haul it off to the park later."

Libby washed the strawberries and pineapple chunks she'd bought for the smoothie drinks and added them back into the refrigerator. She cut up six apples and slipped them in with the pineapple.

The two coffee pots were turned on, one for coffee and one for hot water for tea. She added grounds for her special blend of strong coffee and allowed it to start percolating while the water heated in the other.

"You do this every weekend?" Karen asked.

"No. This is a tournament, so there will be parents arriving from out of the area. If we can sell them hot dogs and snacks and water—they go through pallets of water—"

"I saw those outside. Should I put them in the shade?"

"Good idea. Why don't you fill one of the trays in the refrigerator with some and use one of those beach towels, wet it down, and cover the waters outside to keep them cool?"

Libby wetted down another towel and threw it in the freezer for later on.

"If I'd known, I would have made some sandwiches we could sell."

"We aren't allowed. Anything with mayonnaise or perishable items has to be inspected and cleared by the Health Department. Just heating up hot dogs is fine. I guess we could buy them wrapped at the store. But that defeats the purpose, doesn't it?"

"How about soup?"

"Thank you for reminding me. I have ramen in the car." Libby grabbed her keys and ran to her SUV, covered with the chalk paint on the windows cheering on the Cosmos, Will's soccer team. She brought the ten packages of ramen mixture, stacking them beside the coffee and teapots, so people knew they had a choice.

"Mustard?" Karen asked. "Catsup?"

"In the cupboard above the stove."

Karen washed down both bottles, cleaning the spouts, and set them on the other side of the opening. She found the sugar and creamer and placed them in a dish next to the coffee pot.

"I brought a little half-and-half for snobs. It's in the refrigerator if anyone wants it. I make my coffee strong, so some will ask for milk or will use water to cut it."

"I like it strong," Karen giggled.

Libby filled the refrigerator with more sodas and waters until it was completely full. With two hands doing the work, they got it done in less than the half hour.

"There we go. I think that was the fastest I've ever done that. Thanks, Karen."

"Just wanted to help out. I missed all this part of my childhood. Although when I went out for track in high school, the parents never did this."

Her reveal made Libbie cautious. "I'm sorry, Karen. I'm glad you did track. Coop did too."

"He's a beanpole. I can spot a runner a mile away."

Libby chuckled. "But guess what sport he's best at?"

Karen thought about it for a while and then guessed correctly. "Swimming."

"Amazing. No one ever gets that right. It's because he doesn't float. He glides across the water like a leaf. Makes him very fast."

"I can see that."

"Did your mom remarry?"

"Marry, you mean. She and my father were never married. She was stretched pretty thin, raising me without a husband. She remained single until I was in high school. My grandparents were sick a lot, so she had to help out there too. They had a little ranch there."

"Sounds like you liked it."

"It was great. They had an old horse I got to ride when we visited. We lived with them for a spell before they passed. Grandma was a great cook."

"So does your mother live there at the ranch now?"

"Sadly, no. We were hoping to inherit it someday, but that wasn't in the cards. Grandpa Watson wasn't a very good money manager, and he gambled. When they died, the ranch went to pay their debts and unpaid medical bills."

"I'm sorry for that, Karen." Libby tested the coffee and declared it done. "Don't let me forget to turn that off or it will come out like tar in an hour or two."

Cars started to arrive. Several people bought water bottles, and they sold a pair of coffees.

"So how did you mom meet your dad?" Libby asked.

"I think it was at one of the SEAL parties. She'd been dating some other guy who brought her. They met and liked each other. The other guy deployed and then transferred to Language School, so she was free."

"Love finds a way. I think that's what they say." Libby wasn't yet comfortable but couldn't stop asking questions.

"I have no illusions. I'm a bit like Mom. She never really found that one guy." She smiled, studying her hands and then looked up at Libby. "You're lucky, Libby."

"It will happen for you too, Karen. You just have to be patient. I seem to be quoting all the cliches today, but you know what John Lennon said. 'Life is what happens when you're making other plans.' I think that's the way with love. It comes when you least expect it."

She thought about the day she met Coop. He stood at the front door just like Karen did three days ago. It gave her the chills.

They were joined by Dr. Brownlee and Cooper. Cooper's brow was slightly furled. "You two getting acquainted?"

"Yes," Karen said with a big smile. "Your wife has been showing me the ropes. I think I can successfully run a snack bar now, thanks to Libby."

He grinned. "She's a good teacher." When he winked at Libby, she felt that familiar tingle snake up her spine. It made her blush.

Karen watched the two of them carefully. Austin broke the ice with a question.

"Excuse me, but can I have some coffee?"

Libby's cheeks were still flaming when she served her dad.

One of the other mothers came with her friend. "Libby, you said we could take the first shift. We don't play until noon. Can I spell you?"

"Thank you. I'm so grateful someone actually showed up, I can hardly speak!"

The two ladies took over the space after Libby showed

them the cash drawer and how to replenish everything. She joined Cooper, her dad, and Karen, who had started for the bleachers.

The game was a fun one to watch, mostly because the outcomes were so unpredictable. The youngsters were just learning to control the ball. Some, like Will, were tall. Others were much shorter, and talent was sporadic. Cooper was extremely vocal, so much so Libby reminded him of the time he'd been thrown out of the game because of his comments to the same ref who was officiating the game today.

"Oops," he agreed.

"Oh, you're not hurting anyone, Cooper," Dr. Brownlee added. "You're not yelling at the ref or berating the kids."

But Libby could see Coop was getting worked up again. He wasn't paying attention to their conversation in the stands. He stood, fixated on the boys on the field. When the ref called a foul on Will, Coop lost it. Will had kicked the opposing player in the shin, and the boy fell down on the field. Unless he'd been coached, it probably was a true injury, Libby thought.

"That's not a foul. Get your glasses on ref. He was aiming at the ball, for Chrissakes!"

A whistle was blown, which stopped the game. Cooper immediately sat down, knowing what was to follow.

"Now you've done it," Libby whispered.

Cooper grumbled and kept it to himself.

In black shorts and a black and white striped shirt, the young Hispanic referee came running straight for the stands and stood right in front of Cooper, blowing his whistle again, holding a red card in the air. Then he pointed to the cars in the parking lot. They were Cooper's marching orders. Libby saw Will's coach kick his lawn chair and throw his clipboard, reacting to Cooper's ejection. The down ref blew a whistle, and the coach was ordered off the field as well.

Libby wasn't so afraid of Cooper's feelings as she was Will's. He was mortified. "Dad," he called out. His sweaty forehead already had mud on it, and he was breathing heavy.

She decided to let Cooper stew. She'd only intervene if the coach tried to have words with him, because she knew it wouldn't end well. She decided, if that happened, she'd be in both of their faces and would make sure it stopped.

But the coach picked up his stuff, handed a sheaf of papers to his assistant, another parent, and walked off the field, disappearing.

Of course, the other parents looked at what was left of their little family. She could only guess what they were thinking. They'd lay it on even thicker if they knew, and some of them probably did, what Coop did for a living. Or that her father was a world-renowned authority on PTSD and had pioneered studies on anger and the effects of combat on men and women in the military. Or that they were dealing with a new family member, conceived before a lost relative went off to battle and lost his life. Or that her mother was battling for her life in a bed at home. That she was doing everything she could to hold everyone together.

And, of course, they would never know that, under certain, extreme circumstances, Calvin Cooper could die protecting all of them and would willingly give his life to keep them all safe.

Even the referee.

CHAPTER 19

"YOU WANT TO go have a cup of coffee, Coop?" Dr. Brownlee asked his son-in-law after the game ended. Libby and Karen retreated to the snack bar. Coop wasn't stupid and knew he probably deserved to have the little chat, but he had lost his patience with everything and was on shaky ground. The person he was most upset with was himself. And yes, Brownlee probably knew that. He cared and knew him like a true son. Once, he'd even told Coop he felt he'd always known Cooper even before they met.

He didn't want to play nice, but because Brownlee meant so much to him, to Libby, to his kids, and the whole family, he wanted to be careful. A part of his soul felt dangerous. Maybe it was factored because of the discussion they'd had with Kyle yesterday. He and T.J. were supposed to meet with Tucker and Kelly, even Sven if he was around. He needed to walk into that meeting focused and unemotional.

But the truth was there was no easy, focused way to deal with this issue. Even if it was a non-issue and they all were worrying about something that was never going to happen, he still felt on edge. He felt he needed to fight. Just like Kyle had been fighting for them all these years. Just like Coop tried to defend Will on the soccer field.

He'd have to repair that damage with his son tonight, and he had full confidence he would.

Dammit.

"What do you think, son?" Brownlee's kind eyes matched his soothing voice, polished and practiced from hours and hours of helping tear people off the wall or to step back from the edge. He helped them open up a little window in their hearts to receive some of the miracle of being alive, of being a survivor even though someone close to them was not. The world needed people like Austin Brownlee. It wasn't right to hurt him just because Cooper needed something to punch. That was losing his humanity. He wasn't *that* guy. But he didn't mind being an angry one, either. And if it helped their cause, if he could pass the torch on to these messengers successfully, maybe they could intervene.

"Dad." He rarely used this term out of deference for his father who had died those years ago in the tornado that claimed his whole family. He used it today to let Austin know how special he was. "I have a meeting I have to go to, and I'd like, if you're willing, to table this until that's over with. And then I need to speak to Will. But I would like your help, if you could."

"Sure. Anything, Coop."

"Would you do me the favor of bringing him home after their next game? I may not be done, and besides, I'm not supposed to be on the field."

"Sure. What about Libby?"

"I was supposed to let her clean up and collect the monies. But if you have to get back to—"

"No, that's fine. Count on me. I'll take him for an ice cream after. I'll spoil his dinner, maybe take him to see Carla, and then bring him home."

Cooper nodded, mumbling his thanks.

Dr. Brownlee put his hand on Cooper's forearm. "You're a wonderful father, Coop. But you embarrassed him. And for that, you'll go to Hell."

Cooper had been so wrapped up in his spiraling thoughts he wasn't sure he'd heard the good doctor correctly. He looked up to see Brownlee grinning from ear to ear.

"My mother used to say that to me all the time. I didn't like the joke much then, either. No. You go, and I'll make sure he knows we all are proud of him."

"Thanks," Cooper said as he shook his hand.

He stopped by the snack bar and pulled Libby out to talk to her privately.

"I'm sorry, honey, about the scene I made. I've apologized to your dad, but I'll sit down with Will tonight, I promise, and apologize to him too."

"I thought you knew better, Coop. That was so stupid and really, so unnecessary."

"What can I say? I got triggered. I'm an asshole sometimes. I wouldn't hurt anybody, but I suppose all the parents think I'm an alien or something."

"You're going to have to wait until the rest of the season to earn that back, Cooper. But don't worry about it. Make it right with Will, though. Poor kid. I felt so sorry for him. And then the coach just ripped the hole bigger. Believe it or not, some of the parents started to laugh." She stepped up to touch him with her long torso. "They are just little boys, Coop, only eight or nine. It's not a professional team with any hope to be Olympic players someday. You know there are hills to die on and hills you just ignore. I thought you were over all that."

"I am better than that, but I make mistakes. But tonight, I have to go handle something that was preplanned with T.J. and Tucker. So your dad said he'd bring Will home. Just wanted you to know. I can't stay for the second game anyway. I'm banned for the day."

"But tomorrow…"

"I don't know. See if you can find out. I'm not sure if a red card is one day or the whole tournament. Ask the ref, and tell him I'm sorry."

"Oh boy, here I go again, giving everyone your messages. You know it's not the same as you giving your apology."

"I get it. I can't do it now. But I will. Trust me on this."

She looked up at him, her eyes wide and her lips warm. She had no reproach in her eyes, and he deserved a lot of it too. But Libby was fully behind him.

"Don't be home too late, or will it be?"

"No. Shouldn't take very long. Should I bring something home?"

"More ice cream? Some whipped cream? Be creative." She leaned in and kissed him hard.

"Let's just run away tonight, rent a room, and fuck all night long. Fuck this snack bar, the meeting with T.J., your new cousin, Karen, and everything, okay?"

She laughed and tucked her head under his chin. "Let's discuss it over whipped cream tonight, okay? Maybe we'll come up with a solution. You never know…there are certain things we don't need a motel room for."

She was making it hard to leave, but he had to. "Thanks, Libby. I'll make it up to you. I promise."

She smiled, waved good-bye with her fingers and a coy smile, and assumed her perch inside the snack bar.

"Bye, Karen," he called to her without turning around.

"Bye, Coop," he heard in response.

WHEN HE ARRIVED at the Scupper, T.J. had already downed a beer and was finishing a very sloppy but delicious-smelling double buffalo burger with everything on it, including peppers, onions, even deep-fried oysters. Sven and Kelly were sharing a burger and were drinking red wine. Tucker had yet to arrive.

He ordered a shrimp salad. T.J. looked up from his bloody mess and growled, his hands dripping with catsup and meat juice. A thin rivulet of fat dribbled down his chin.

"How was the game? Your kid plays football, right?" Sven asked.

"Well, he's nine. He thinks he does." He thanked the waitress for his mineral water, took a sip, and continued. "We had a little incident today on the field, and I got tossed from the game."

Sven began to clap. Kelly was laughing.

"You see, that's how we play in Europe. Sometimes, at the sidelines, you hear like ten different languages spewing all of the most disgusting and filthy swear words out there. The kids who play international learn all their teammates' words within weeks of being on the team."

Coop stopped him. "Sven, wake up. My kid is nine. I'm not going to have him swearing until he's at least eleven, got it?"

Kelly spit out her wine.

T.J. wiped his fingers on a shred of napkin left. "Geez, Coop. You're in a mood."

Cooper pressed several napkins into T.J.s chest.

"Thanks."

Kelly leaned forward. "How was your mission, Cooper? T.J. said you rescued about ten girls. Good for you!"

"I call it a success. That's partly what I want to talk to you guys about. But I want to wait for Tucker."

They both nodded, becoming serious.

"How did New York go?"

"The ambassador doesn't know what he's doing. He should have had me do his briefings. He's been eating the pablum State prepares for him. Their intel has really gone downhill. I made some introductions, told him who to watch out for, and who he should not negotiate with. He was surprised when I told him the ambassador from Nigeria is from a slave-trading family and very proud of it. They have a big monument in front of their office building erected to one of their ancestors who calls himself "King of the Slaves." Now his distant grandson is on the Human Rights Commission. Isn't that rich?"

"The monument is still up there?" Cooper asked. "I think I saw some of those when we were in Benin. The *Point of No Return* shrines."

"The last places slaves would see their land. Who does that? Takes people, sells them like cattle, and then makes them walk through a gauntlet like that, where people stand on the sides and taunt them. How does a country heal from that?"

"Not while the monuments are still out there. They give lip service to the whole problem. They dress well, drink expensive wines, pretend they are cultured, and make a profit off the sale of human flesh."

"So he's still in the trade?" T.J. asked.

"They never gave it up. They've morphed and do it underground. All the while, they maintain a museum to the slave trade, telling their story to tourists who come back to Africa to see their roots. These people sold their ancestors and then sell tickets to the descendants of today who come visit. That's wrong in so many ways."

The discussion would have been a morbid one, except that the more Kelly spoke, the more hopeful Coop was that she could perhaps effect some change for Kyle or find out what was going on.

Tucker walked in. "Sorry, guys. Just before I was going to walk out of the house, the baby threw up all over me. It was so bad I had to take a shower too."

Tucker bumped fists with everyone there and saluted Kelly.

"What will you have? It's on me," Coop said.

"Nah, we ate already. And I can't stay too long. Brandy is pretty frazzled these days."

"Good. Okay." A waitress arrived, and Cooper ordered Tucker a beer. "So T.J. and I wanted to speak with you about something that's going on with Team 3. And, Kelly, we really missed you this last time. I'm not sure what you heard about it."

"Just what T.J. told me. You rescued ten girls from a Catholic college near L.A. All safe, but I heard some were—" She motioned with her hand, wabbling it back and forth.

"Unfortunately, yes. We were sent originally to pick up a known bad guy, Rufus Denaro, but the mission changed when he wasn't present when we went back for the girls. Originally, we were to leave the girls there and a Mexican team was coming in to retrieve them. Then we were told to just get them out of there and get Rufus if he was there."

"That's a tall order, Cooper. Interpol has been after this guy for three years now. He has connections all over Eastern Europe. They're starting to take young Muslim girls from Turkey and Syria, bring them North, and then smuggle them out of Amsterdam for England and the States. Some of the buyers consider it a rescue, if you can believe such a thing."

"I imagine you have families willing to sell."

"Oh, sure. People are disappearing all the time, especially the young girls. Parents are being told, just like the poor families in Central America, that their daughters will go to wealthy American and English businessmen who will house them in castles and skyscrapers and one day they'll help the parents escape as a thank you. All lies. None of it is true. There are very high suicide rates amongst these girls, who soon realize it's all a sham and cannot bring themselves to live that way. These guys are the worst. I heard they were in Mexico, too, but not Baja. That's the Cortez cartel territory."

"And maybe that's the problem, Kelly. Maybe you can help us with this. I'm bothered by the fact that, at first, this guy Rufus was there. We actually saw him there at the ranch. And then he wasn't. They auctioned those girls off on a low frequency television station that plays mariachi music. Had it all set up like one of those shopping channels."

"Ballsy. In Cortez backyard too. Although they're having their share of problems."

"We were given intel that this Rufus guy was a big player moving into Baja. And they wanted him out."

"To help the competition," Kelly said.

"No shit," Tucker said.

"Well, at State, we make alliances with whomever advances our U.S. interests."

"But what would they want with a drug cartel who also smuggles girls? American girls. What possible alliance could that provide?" Coop asked.

"That's an interesting question. We don't always know about all the deals Washington does. Just like us supporting this 'King of Slaves' guy. Helping him get on the council was a power move to keep someone else out. I usually look for the missing piece, like in a puzzle. That's the easiest to find, but you have to have all the other pieces in place first."

What she was saying was true.

"So you figure someone from our side leaked to Denaro about the raid? Aided in his escape?"

"Well, he got away with his life, but that's not much of a save," Kelly answered. "The merchandise was stolen right from under him."

"What if all he wanted was the money from the auction?" asked T.J.

Kelly nodded her head. "Possible. He's got the money and doesn't have to transport them. But someone wanted those girls."

"Cortez cartel?" Tucker asked.

"I think they are your source for the leak on Rufus's location. They don't want him moving into Baja California. Besides, it works with all their ships, the access to all that ocean. They have a perfect location. They can smuggle by land, by air, and by sea. Baja is like Smuggler's Island in the Bahamas a century and a half ago."

"That would explain the notification to the U.S. authorities. We've been working with Cortez for years, right?" Coop remarked.

"Yes. He's been helpful for solving some of the drug crime on the mainland. He's given us good intel, especially with roving bands of militia preying on tourists and that horrible church massacre of those Mormon missionaries," she added. "For that, we'd turn a blind eye on some things, but this, this is way bigger than intel. It's on such a large scale that we'd be looking good if we could come up with this guy. The U.S. would earn lots of creds to capture him alive. He's wanted in nearly a dozen countries. But never here, where he did this."

"So what am I missing, Kelly?" Coop asked.

"I don't know. It doesn't make sense. I'd have to do some digging around. I have to be very careful about that, especially since someone wants to protect this guy for some reason. Depending on who that is, it could be dangerous."

"Do you think it could be someone from our own government?" Tucker asked.

"They're only powerful enough to enter into this because they have the backing of someone big outside. Someone whose name you never hear, who doesn't have office hours, and who never runs for anything public. It might be a syndicate, not a person at all, but it's feeding some 'waiters,' let's say, who bring them the food. That's what it looks like to me."

Sven spoke up, asking a question. "Cooper, why is all this important? You saved the girls. You guys will eventually get Rufus if you're sent back in enough times. Or they'll ask you to roll out and abandon the plan. The public wants to see an end to the trafficking, so that won't happen, but your jobs are secure. You just do what you're told. So why all the questions?"

Both Tucker and T.J. looked at Cooper, who had the answer. "Because they're maybe trying to toss Kyle from the Teams. Punish him for the death of three Mexican nationals and someone who was working undercover for the CIA, perhaps dual citizenship."

"Kyle was told this?" Sven asked. "Those fuckers."

"Exactly!" said Tucker, clinking his beer with T.J.

"He was told there's a negative report going up the line, being edited. When that report gets turned in, Collins says Kyle might lose his job."

He let that sink in.

"I don't know this Collins guy well enough to give an answer for you. But from what I'm hearing, they could be trying to set Kyle up, maybe make him do or say something he wouldn't otherwise do or possibly using the killings as the reason when all they need is to turn him. Then again, maybe they really want him out. Want to replace him with someone they can control."

Kelly's words fell hard on the table.

"So there's only one person who has the kind of clout to find out about this shit, Kelly. That's your father-in-law," Tucker said.

Kelly nodded. "Is this what you want, Cooper?"

"We're trying to protect Kyle. He's the innocent one. He's gone to bat for all of us, saved many lives, kept this team as the effective unit it is."

"Legendary," added T.J.

"He can't ask this, but those of us here who know him best want to do it outside the lines, back channel. We think you and Riley might be able to do that for us. It's either that or wait for them to pressure or hang him. And I don't want to be on this team when I have to serve under someone other than Kyle."

Kelly stood up. "Okay, give me a day. I'm gonna take the jet up to Portland and speak to him tomorrow. If he's out, I can't help you either. If he tells me to stand down, I will have to comply. Understood?"

"Yes. Even knowing that would help. He has to understand he's helping perhaps some of his future employees. We don't have to be boy scouts forever, Kelly."

She smiled. "I'm sure he'll like hearing that. But don't tease if you can't deliver."

"Given time, Kelly, who knows? But it might take time.

Not that we couldn't start funneling some good fits his way."

"And that would be the second-best solution. Okay, I got it. Now I have to go set it up. He likes to figure things out before I get there, so when I walk off the plane, he's going to present me a roadmap. I'll have to fill in some of the blanks, of course. But it's like doing a jigsaw puzzle to him, like what I told you before. No promises, but let me see what we can do."

"Thanks, ma'am." Coop said, standing and leaning over the table to shake her hand. "Godspeed."

She led Sven out of the Scupper like he was tethered by a leash.

In a way, he was, Coop thought.

CHAPTER 20

LIBBY HEARD COOPER'S Hummer drive up and park. The kids had showered and gone to bed early. She was choosing what she should tell her husband. She'd spent the day with Karen, and she had to admit she was developing some ties with her, and it did feel sort of natural. She was careful but trusted her instincts, and her instincts told her Karen was the real deal.

But there was more on the horizon, and that's what she had to discuss with Coop. Plus, she didn't want to interfere with his promise; he'd make it up to Will. She'd have to wait to see which man it was who came home to her tonight. That was always the problem. She had to remain flexible because the man who walked in through that front door might not be the same one who left.

And she loved both those men, embraced and supported them.

She heard the latch turn. She had candles on in the bedroom, and she was freshly showered and wearing a silk nightgown that was partially see-through.

But taking one look at him, she knew that wasn't what he

was looking for tonight.

Okay, Plan B.

He walked toward her, the warm glow of the candles softening the lines on his face and making the tufts of unruly hair on the top of his head appear to be on fire. He watched as her breathing made the silk gown rise and fall, noticed how her nipples knotted up just because he was looking at them under the fabric. He placed a hand over her left breast, over her heart.

"Sweetheart, I want to be here with you tonight, just like this. This is so perfect. Now I won't be able to sleep. But I gotta take care of Will. I promised, and you probably told him that, right?"

She inhaled and told him the truth. "Yes, I did."

He held her jaw with his callused palm, the stubby fingers with cuts and gashes all over them, fingers that had done things she didn't want to think about, but that also pleasured her in ways she could never get enough of. Just the feel of those fingers drifting down her body was enough to send her into pre-orgasm.

His thumb brushed against her lips. "Tell me you understand. And you agree I'm doing the right thing."

"You are. I'll have to wait. I'll look forward to your full attention, Coop. I promise to give you right back everything I've got, baby." She kissed him, her tongue lingering against his, teasing him to go deeper, and he did.

His moan was almost painful to hear. His hands gripped her ass, pressing her into his groin. The stubble of his beard made her neck and cheeks tingle afterwards. The trail of his tongue left a lasting brand on her flesh.

"How did I get so lucky, Libby? How in the world did that happen? I don't deserve you."

"Of course, you did. It was perfect, our meeting. Perfect in every way. If it weren't for Uncle Will's sacrifice, I might not have ever met you."

"Oh, yes, we would have met. I feel so strongly about that," he said with his forehead pressed against hers. "I'd have seen you on the street, and I would have known instantly my life had changed. You taught me about love, Libby. You helped me heal. You gave me family and a future."

"So go deal with your son, your family. He loves you so much. You are still a god to him, even when he's angry at you. You are the most important person in his life, Coop."

She watched him walk down the hall and open up the closet where he had some camping equipment. He grabbed the blue nylon pack that contained the two-man tent they'd bought with some of their wedding money. It was a first-class French tent, lightweight and warm.

Closing the closet door, he tiptoed out to the backyard and quietly put the tent up. Then he lit the interior with a lamp, and set down two sleeping bags, unzipped, lying on top of each other.

She would have gladly gone with him into the tent, but that wasn't his plan. He walked into Will's room, filled with pictures of race cars and rocket ships, even some Navy SEAL promotion photographs. Sitting on the edge of the bed, he woke his son up.

"Oh, Dad, I'm sorry I yelled at you. I thought maybe you

were mad at me."

"No, son. Never think that. I love you. I'm so sorry I embarrassed you today. I won't let it happen again."

"But we won. We move on tomorrow. We're in second place, Dad. Nick, Cody's dad, coached us, and we played great. He let me play keeper, Dad. I loved it."

"Really? I thought you liked to run—"

"But I can kick. I'm the best kicker on the team. And I can throw the ball. Keepers get to throw the ball to their teammates."

"Good for you. So you won both games?"

"Yes, that's what I'm telling you."

"Gosh, I didn't know that when I left. No one told me."

"I don't think Grandpa knew. He doesn't really have a clue for soccer. He's nice, but he doesn't do sports."

"Tennis. That's a sport. And golf."

Will's nose wrinkled. He noticed Libby standing in the doorway.

"Hey, sweetheart. I didn't tell him because I wanted you to."

Cooper turned, surveying the lines of her body one more time. "Can I request a couple of mugs of hot chocolate for the cold night air?"

"Absolutely."

Libby prepared the chocolate in the oversized mugs she usually reserved for soup. She piled whipped cream on top and added some chocolate sprinkles, presenting it to her two men standing in the living room, barefoot.

"Holy cow, Mom!"

“Thanks, sweetheart,” Coop said, kissing her cheek. Turning to Will, he asked, “You want me to carry you across the lawn? I put the tent up so we could do a campout.”

“I’ll wear my flip-flops.” He set his chocolate down and ran to his room, returning with his zoris.

Coop put a gentle arm around him. “You’ll have to help me. I’m much older than you, and I have sore joints.”

“No problem, Dad. I’ll hold you up. Just don’t spill your chocolate.”

And off they went. Coop looked back at her one more time before he zipped the tent closed. She could still see their shadows in the light and hear them talking about things only dads and their sons do when they are camping out in their own backyards at night.

She knew Will would tell her tomorrow it was super-secret stuff.

THEY ALL ARRIVED at the soccer field together the next morning. Karen wasn’t there, but the work wasn’t difficult since they’d put everything away neatly last night. She got the coffee started, moved the pallets of cold drinks back outside, and checked to make sure they had the refrigerator fully stocked. There was going to be a chance that it would be hotter today, and the games could go all day long, especially if there had to be sudden death playoffs.

One of the hired refs posted the standings on the wall of the snack bar. She studied where the Cosmos stood.

They were in an easier flight. A very competitive traveling team from a private boys’ school were highly favored. The

Cosmos were not expected to beat these boys, and everyone knew it, but Will's team needed to come out in first place in their bracket today in order for the privilege to play the Blue Rays in the finals. Making it to the finals was what Will was hoping for. She overheard parents talking the same. Some even stated that yesterday, while it started out so rocky, was actually one of the best times their boy had had.

The team walked out on the field like a winning team. They were confident. Their tall boys looked even taller. Their little ones ran around in circles, practicing ball handling like they were putting on an exhibition. They didn't look anything like the team who'd showed up yesterday morning.

Libby missed some of the action as she stayed in the snack bar but heard lots of cheering from their side of the field. The old coach shouted commands from the bench, and the assistant coach actively participated as well. At one point, she saw the coach salute Cooper.

Apparently, the hatchet had been buried.

Libby saw her dad helping her mother out of the car and walk slowly towards the field. She waved. Libby had not expected this. Her mom was bundled up with a hat, mittens, and her big after-ski boots. She wore her white parka with the faux fur trim. She looked good in white. Her color was radiant.

"Mom," she said as she came out of the box to hug her. "Nice to see you. Will is playing now, so you both should get to the bleachers. See Cooper?"

"Will do. Couldn't let my grandson down."

"He'll love seeing you."

Cooper helped her maneuver up the stairs to find a perch

next to him on the top rung. Her father sat on the other side of Coop, who put his arm around her mom and whispered something about the game, pointing at the field.

The boys played hard, and Will was responsible for several saves. The other team had several boys who could kick hard, but their accuracy was failing. Will's team was better with challenging the ball, since they'd spend most their practice on learning how to steal the ball from another player. It paid off.

The assistant coach's son scored a goal, and the crowd went nuts.

Libby scanned the parking lot, looking for Karen. She finally spotted her, walking with the woman Libby knew to be her mother. It had all been arranged before she even knew her own mother was going to show up. She and Karen both decided just to bring both sides of the family together and let them mix however they could. They discussed various schemes to do this, and in the end, they just resigned themselves to let the family members do whatever they felt comfortable doing. And they'd call it perfect.

Karen's smiling face was a younger version of her mother's, who also was an attractive woman. She was very short in comparison to her tall daughter.

"Mom, this is Libby Brownlee-Cooper, Dad's niece."

"Hello, Libby. Nice to meet you," she said. "I'm Melissa Murphy. Thank you for allowing Karen to join you, for being so nice to her."

"We've enjoyed manning the snack bar. Kind of a fun and unexpected way to get acquainted."

They heard a roar from the bleachers.

"Will's team is playing right now. You don't want to miss any of it. My dad and Cooper and, as a surprise even to me, my mother came today."

"Karen's told me about her surgery. I hope things go well for her. It's nice that she's able to get out so soon."

"Yes, I think it's her first time. Do you want anything from the snack bar?"

"No, dear. Thanks, though. We had a huge pancake breakfast, and I'm sorry that caused us to be late."

"They'll have another game, and then, fingers crossed, they'll play in the finals if they come out first in their bracket."

"Goodness. Exciting," Karen's mom said.

Karen led her up to the top seat and took up a place beside Coop, introducing her mother. They were in the process of shaking hands and making further introductions when the other team scored a goal against Will's team. Will had missed protecting the box.

The whistle blew, indicating it was halftime. The score was tied at one-all. Several parents congregated around the snack bar, ordering coffee and tea, granola bars, and water.

Libby kept her eye on the little crowd at the top of the bleachers. Her mother had put on her sunglasses, which covered half her face, and was not smiling.

For a brief moment, Libby thought perhaps they'd made a huge miscalculation. Libby saw her father stand up, come over to Karen, and meet her mother. She reacted by putting both her hands on her cheeks and, although it was difficult to tell, appeared to blush. Libby's mother continued to look out onto the field, expressionless, off in another world. Her heart began to break.

She was helping a group of players purchase water and granola bars, when she noticed Cooper had brought her mother over to the snack bar. She was not a happy camper.

"Libby, you owe me an explanation. I didn't get myself out of bed to meet the slut that slept with your uncle Will. And you thought I would just welcome her with open arms. Have you gone crazy?"

"Mom, it's not like that. Karen is a blood relation to me."

"Well, that woman is not. And did you hear what she told your father?"

"Of course not, Mom. I'm too far away."

Cooper stood motionless, studying the ground. He was going to stay out of it if he could.

"She said, *'Oh my! It's just like seeing a ghost. You look so much like him. And just as handsome as he was as a younger man. You take my breath away, Doctor.'* Isn't that the most ridiculous thing you've ever heard? Where do they get these people? He must have met her at a bar."

"Carla, come on," Cooper started.

He would learn his lesson soon, Libby thought.

"They aren't here to make any demands on you. They just want to meet the family. Karen's grown up her whole life wondering what that family looked like, who they were."

"Well, that's not my fault. I didn't get your father pregnant before we got married. Just because she has loose morals, she has no right to bring all that into our family."

"Mom, listen to me." Libby turned her. "Cooper and I had sex before we were married too. If he'd gone off on a deployment, that could very well have been what happened to me. Don't think I would not have chosen to have the baby, because I wouldn't do that. When he left, we liked each other, but we hadn't decided to get married. It could have easily happened to us."

"Why wasn't I told?"

"I didn't think you'd be here, Mom. But now that you are, I'm glad. Just talk to her. Be nice. Karen's been very nice to work with. She helped me all day yesterday. If I didn't feel some sort of connection with her, my cousin—"

"That has yet to be proven. We've not seen the DNA test analysis."

"Sure, we can do that. But isn't it obvious?" Coop inserted himself. "She recognized Austin right away. I believe her, and I believe Karen. But if you choose not to have anything to do with her, well, that's your choice. That doesn't mean we can't."

"You'd do that to me? In my present condition?"

"All right. I'll agree springing this on you was probably a mistake," Libby answered. "But we didn't know. We brought her here to introduce her to Will, our son, and to Dad. We didn't figure it would hurt. But no one is making you do anything you don't want to do."

Carla looked between Libby and Coop.

Coop stooped to whisper his message to her. "Would you like for me to take you home? I'll do that if you like."

"No. I came to see Will play soccer. I'm staying for that. Help me back," she said to Cooper.

The second half was about to begin. When the players came out on the field, the Brownlee contingent was loud.

Melissa whistled and screamed, "Go Cosmos!"

Libby started to giggle. Her mother was so used to being the center of attention, and at parties, she'd always been such a larger-than-life character that she loved the interaction and made everyone in her presence have a wonderful time.

Now she was struggling to show an appropriate emotion. Maybe she had been unfair about all of this.

When the ball was kicked hard right into Will's stomach, he fell and appeared to be lying there immobile. Then he got up, having the wind knocked out of him. His team defended the box until he could run towards the player who kicked the ball so hard the first time. Will landed on the ball, covering it fully, even absorbing a kick that hit him in the shoulder.

A whistle blew, and the game was stopped. The other player was charged with a foul, and because it was within the goalkeeper's area, a penalty kick was allowed. The coach was going to pick the assistant coach's son to make the kick, and the assistant overruled him. They chose Will.

He touched the ball after the whistle, stepped back one step, and drilled it into the upper right corner of the net of the opposing team for a goal.

Even Libby's mother was on her feet, cheering. Coop turned around and slipped Libby a thumbs-up. Maybe all wasn't forgiven just yet, she thought, but the winter thaw had begun. And that was a very good sign.

CHAPTER 21

COOPER HAD TAKEN Kyle out to breakfast, which was a mistake because they hadn't gotten their workout in yet.

"You sure you wouldn't just want to go back to bed and forget this fine breakfast, Coop? You could start your day over in another hour or two."

"Not on your life. You're my LPO, and I'm taking good care of you."

"Well, for now anyway."

"I wish you wouldn't say that. Colin Riley is going to at least help find out what's happened. Someone's dirty. I can just feel it. Can't you?"

"I don't know what I feel any longer. You get to a point where you start to think you're being followed, maybe your phone's been tapped. I just feel like a big fuckin' target. I never felt that way before."

"Do you think you could be followed?"

"No. I'm just saying that. It's like when you wake up from a dream and you imagine something happened when it really didn't. But it seems real when you wake up. You would swear someone spoke to you a certain way—you know what I mean."

"No. I don't feel that way, Kyle. Have you had this discussion with Christy?"

"No, but I better. She's started talking about taking more time off. We're going to make sure this is our last, so she says she wants to enjoy it. Maybe take six months off. And that will be hard if I'm out of a job and haven't been here long enough to collect my pension." He shook his head. "All those long, hard years. What do I have to show for it? I'm going to have to have my hip replaced sometime in the next five years. My shoulders are busted up. I can feel arthritis starting in my fingers."

"Now you're talking like an ordinary grunt. You're no ordinary guy, Kyle, and you know it. I don't want to hear you speaking like this. Seriously. It's not good for you."

He nodded, staring out the window as if looking for something to go run and accomplish. That was Kyle. Always moving. Coop thought the idea of him not being able to do what they did on the Teams was probably more packed with horror than even thoughts of death. Not everyone would understand that, but Coop did. And they'd both seen strong men—men full of principles, who did heroic things—get melted down by society and their lack of discipline. They lose their guidepost. Some of them weren't able to go it alone. And the first thing that happened was they begin to question if they've done any good at all. That's what Kyle was sounding like.

"Sounds like I need to tell Christy. She'll whip my ass." He grinned and finished his orange juice. "Nicely," he said as he wiggled his eyebrows.

"That's probably a better plan. She's got your back, your kids, your soul, and your dick. Nobody better to set you straight with all your priorities. She's only working hard because you give it your all. Trust me, that's why she's with you. Don't give up on the dream. You owe her that."

"I do. What bothers me is I don't see many who are happy afterwards, and yeah, I guess that does scare me a little. Some become hugely successful, even billionaires. Private jets, hanging out with Senators, and such."

"They aren't our crowd, Kyle. You got to have an ego the size of Texas to pull that off. James Bond? A legend in your own mind? That's horseshit, man."

"Okay, I get you. But still, there are some that—"

"You'll find something else. Speaking of private jets, what about working for Colin Riley?"

"I thought about it. But I'm putting it out of my mind until I know for sure."

"There you go. See, you can put one thing out of your mind. Why can't you put that fear out there in the garbage heap too? He'd get you something right away. Don't worry about it, Kyle."

"You're probably right. Okay. Well, we're not quitting today, so let's go bust our stomachs at Gunny's."

Cooper was happy with that reaction.

The gym was empty on a Monday, which was a bit unusual. But there were lots of end of school events going on, and the tourist season was picking up in San Diego. Many men had people visiting this time of year because it was so mild and yet still warm. Outside of things Coop had seen in the Florida

Keys, San Diego was one of the prettiest places on the planet.

Timmons was unloading supplies from his van.

"You want some help with that, old man?" Kyle yelled out.

"Shut the fuck up. Get your ass back on that machine," Timmons retorted without thinking. He had a load that was crowned by a large bundle of toilet paper, a twenty-four pack, and it bounced and wobbled from side to side before finally spilling over the glass countertop and onto the floor behind.

Coop and Kyle moved to the next machine, the leg press. Kyle was really pushing his limit today.

"Hey, Kyle, what the hell happened to Collins?" Timmons asked, speaking about the man who replaced him after his retirement.

"What do you mean?" Kyle asked.

"He's gone. He got axed. Something about an IRS audit. Some non-reported income. You ever hear about some investment he had in Mexico?"

Kyle and Cooper looked at each other. Coop began to get excited that perhaps their worries were over.

"We had no clue, Timmons. Who did you hear that from?" Coop wondered.

"It's in the base paper. Got his picture and everything. He was taking bribes and spent it on a condo in Mexico he bought with cash. Taking bribes is illegal per the Navy, but the IRS still wants to get their taxes, and since he didn't report the cash, he got nailed."

"Let me see that," Kyle said as he grabbed the paper from Timmons' hands.

Cooper read over his shoulder. The article went on to say

that Collins had found himself in debt due to a recent divorce. "He invested in a condo complex in Cabo San Lucas, built by Carlos Rosas, a dual citizen whose development company did a lot of government contracts on military bases and facilities near the border."

"You think that's the guy who was at that party?" Coop asked.

"I don't know. The dual citizen thing catches the eye, though, doesn't it?"

"Sure does."

"I never liked that guy," Timmons said. "I'd almost gotten all my stuff out, told him I'd be back after the weekend, and the jerk just chucked my stuff."

"Not one of your frogs, I hope." Team 3 had bought Timmons a series of glass frogs posing with a surfboard. The statues were highly fragile, and several times, Timmons had gotten overheated and kicked his file cabinet and the thing would fall on the floor and break. They'd had to replace it, at last count, four times.

"No. I broke it moving out of my house, not the office." He pointed to the green statue in the display case in front of him. "I glued this one back together."

The bright green frog had been the brunt of so many jokes with the team, until they helped Timmons move his things out of his house when his wife divorced him. She had the living room and all the bedrooms filled with glass cases with her doll collection. Every time Master Chief (now retired) Timmons had walked through his front door, he went from the real world where he made a big difference in the lives of young men under his influence, men he gave his best for even though he wasn't in combat any longer, and he entered a world of make believe, where he mattered not at all. It broke Coop's heart to see that.

Adele had taken everything he had. All the furniture, not that he'd want that garbage, the two cars, but mostly his dignity. She let him keep his beater truck. She never saw the hero in him. She even tried to take away his retirement and his relationship with his daughter, Cassie.

"Did you ever get he was doing anything like this illegal?" Kyle asked.

"No. He wasn't very social. He had a good friend who was a private dick, who worked divorce cases and such. After the divorce, he was kind of a loner. But he did go on vacation a lot. I remember people complaining about him not being around as much as I was. I didn't mind the compliment. But I just never liked him. Something not right about him, especially for a SEAL."

"Maybe it had something to do with that mission he fucked up," Coop asked.

"Who knows? Anyway, good riddance. My understanding is they're downgrading the post, making it more administrative."

The two of them opted for a cappuccino afterwards. The news about Collins was surprising, but it still didn't solve the problem Kyle faced. Coop was curious about where that supposedly damaging report was filed, though.

"Let's call Kelly," said Cooper.

"I got it." Kyle dialed the number. "Hey, Kelly, this is Kyle

Lansdowne. We were just given an interesting piece of news. Collins has been fired. Is that true?"

"You didn't hear anything from me, but apparently, Senator Burns launched a probe into Collins' financial affairs and found the discrepancies between cash he used to buy a condo and what he reported to the IRS. They also found a Mexican bank account he didn't report with half a million of what they think is Uncle Sam's money."

"Geez, that asshole. He scrimped on us too, then."

"Definitely. He'll be put away for quite some time. Some of the money was being siphoned off, earmarked for the Teams, but never got there. Some of it was spent on equipment that was shipped but disappeared. He was connected to a cartel from Monterey hoping to expand to Baja California, right in the area where your last mission was. What a coincidence. Did you ever get wind of such a thing?"

"Hell no," Kyle answered.

"I think your mission helped them put the puzzle pieces together, Kyle. Congratulations. I think you'll be getting a promotion, at least a raise."

"No kidding. I'd heard Collins had a report—"

"There's no report that they found, and if there ever was, it's a pile of ash. Senator Burns is most grateful for your service. Your Team is to be recommended for a special commendation."

After Kyle hung up, his only comment was, "Well, holy hell. I guess I was worried about nothing, then."

"I never put much stock in it, Kyle. I knew you were in the clear all along. We just had to find a way to prove it. Was only a matter of time. When it comes down to it, the bad guys aren't very smart, are they?"

"You're damn right. Otherwise, they'd be good guys and do it the right way."

"Hoo-Ya, Chief Lansdowne."

"Hoo-Ya, and thank you, Coop. Now what do I owe you for this kind breakfast gesture as well as the great advice?"

Cooper had one thing he wondered about, so he decided to let Kyle know. "You know that KA-BAR knife I have, the one given to me at my Trident ceremony, that had Medic Will Brownlee's name engraved on the blade?"

"Yeah. You still have it?"

"Yes, I do. I wouldn't part with it for anything. Someday, it's going to my son, Will. But I was wondering, can we get another one of those made?"

"How come?"

"Turns out Will fathered a child he never knew he had, or rather, he died before she was born and never met her. She's just come here, seeking to learn about Will and his family. It's a funny twist of fate, isn't it? I came here for the very same reason. I stood right there in the Brownlee foyer and spoke to Libby for the first time, just like Karen did over a week ago. We've gotten acquainted with her, and she's okay people. We've even met her mom, Will's friend before he left for Grenada. I don't want to give her my KA-BAR, but I'd like to give her one for herself. If we can do that."

"Coop, consider it done. One way or the other, we'll have one made. I don't know if they'll officially sanction it, but we'll get 'er done. And I'll let you present it to her yourself."

"Thanks, Kyle." Cooper was overcome with emotion, but he inhaled twice, and the moisture in his eyes dissipated.

"You okay?"

At first, Coop couldn't speak. He nodded until his voice returned. "Who would have thought when you sent me on that mission, after I'd lost my family, that I'd find a whole new family? When Will's daughter showed up at our doorstep, at first, I wasn't sure. But then I knew. That's how we honor Will and the sacrifice he made for all of us. It wasn't fair that he left us. It broke a lot of hearts and changed a lot of lives. He never got to experience what Libby's dad got to experience, what I've been blessed with. But we honor the fallen by living well and remembering his name."

"Living and loving well. Forgiveness. Redemption. Honor and strength. Raising families who learn to love this country and treat her people with respect. That's the real job, isn't it?"

"Yup. That's who we are. Great to be serving with you, Kyle. Hope to do it all the way to my twenty, maybe more."

"Me too. Me too."

CHAPTER 22

Six Months Later

LIBBY SAT WITH her mom for her regular monthly checkup. She looked especially pretty today, having bought a new wig, a short bob that resembled how she used to wear her hair when she was first married. Her dad said he liked it.

"You feeling better?" Libby asked.

"You know, I feel like I'm getting stronger. And I so look forward to these two weeks between my treatments. I'm really getting tired of the technicolor throwing ups. Depending on the drug, I never know what I'm going to see in the toilet bowl. But when I get a little break, like this, I feel normal."

She looked down at her blouse, hanging flat against her nearly concave chest.

"It will come. First things first."

"Your dad is a real gentleman. He lets me keep a tee shirt on when I feel up to a little friskiness. But he never lets his hands stray down here. He never forgets, even though we try to pretend we're young and we'll both live forever. The man has been such a blessing."

"That's how you know someone really loves you," added

Libby, her eyes getting moist.

Carla blinked her eyelashless eyelids until her tears disappeared.

"You know, you were right about Karen. Your dad's kind of a little taken by her, I think." She smiled, but it wasn't filled with animosity like before. Libby was pleased her mom had settled in and was so accepting of the family addition. "I even sort of like her mom, except I still don't like the way she looks at Austin."

"Did we do the right thing, Mom? Forcing everyone together?"

"Like you had a choice, you mean? No, that's not the kind of family we are. Even Marsha's been writing letters, real nice letters, and the girls are sending pictures, drawings of me that, well, frankly make me look like Frankenstein, but—" She started to laugh. "I should walk into a family reunion topless, shouldn't I?"

Libby pressed her palm against her mouth. She was equally divided between the pain of her mom's joke and the pure gallows humor of it.

"I'm not going to wager on that."

"You shouldn't. I might be less of a woman, I might not have tits, but I still have my spirit."

"You still have a nice ass. I heard Dad say that the other day."

"Oh, you shouldn't have told me about that." She smiled, wrapping her arms around her torso. "Oh, what a picture that would be. Can you see the grandkids' faces if I came walking onto the patio naked, with good legs and a fine ass and a front that looked like I'd had a run-in with an airplane propeller?"

Libby giggled in spite of herself. "You have to stop this. I'm going to pee my pants."

"Well, that will make two of us." Carla glanced around the room. "Wonder what's taking Dr. Nashua so long." She leaned closer to Libby and whispered. "I'll bet she has a new patient she has to talk to, you know, someone having a hard time dealing with the realities of their cancer."

"Probably."

Just then, the door opened, and the pretty Egyptian doctor entered followed by Dr. Green.

"Oh my, we have the welcoming committee here today!" Carla announced.

"You look great, Carla," Dr. Green said as he shook her hand. Dr. Nashua nodded to a chair at the side.

"Please, Dr. Green, take a chair."

Libby's heart began to beat wildly. She watched every movement Dr. Nashua made, the way she cleared her throat, licked her lips, quickly inhaled when she laid out on her desk a small pile of white papers. Reports.

No, God, please no!

"Carla, I'm afraid I have some bad news. That's why I waited because I wanted Dr. Green here for this discussion."

Carla was frozen in place. She gave the doctor a death stare, an art she'd practiced well. Libby could see it immediately made Dr. Nashua nervous.

"We got back your latest scan and the results of your blood work, and I'm afraid we're fighting new battles every month, it seems, and from what I'm reading here, we're losing the battle."

Carla swallowed hard then her hand shot out and grabbed Libby's.

"My concern is for your quality of life."

"Well, life is the operative word, isn't it, doctor?" Carla said tersely.

"Of course. And that's always been foremost. But every test, we find new issues coming up, new things we have to address. You are spending half your time being very sick from the chemo, and although you've never complained, it can't be bringing you much joy."

"I wouldn't put it like that, not unless you're a graphic artist and looking for inspiration in the designs I'm making in the bottom of a toilet bowl."

Libby squeezed her hand, which had gotten very cold.

"But the fact is you're not getting better. The cancer is spreading. We can keep this regimen you're on for a few months, but each month, it's going to deliver a nasty punch to your system. It will make you weaker, less able to fight off infections and less able to kick your immune system into help with your overall health."

"I do drink a lot of fresh beet and kale juices. Those are supposed to help the drugs and help my own cells regenerate."

"And I think, when I look at you, all that's working, Mrs. Brownlee. Your coloring is wonderful. Your hair is even beginning to grow back."

Libby's mom pulled her wig off. "It's not my real hair, doctor. It's a wig." Her new hair, coming in quite white, was developing in swirls, a little curly, looking more like feathers sticking out of her scalp here and there. Carla's face was expressionless.

"Carla, we knew that's a wig," Dr. Green interjected. "She meant you no disrespect, please. Just hear her out, and then we can discuss a few things."

"Yes, I apologize if I came—"

"No, I understand. I take no offense. I mean, look at what's been done to me. I'm grateful for all the attempts you have made, extreme attempts even, to help me survive this. But what you're saying is it's not enough. I am losing this battle, right?"

Dr. Nashua answered her, with her palms together on the desk in front of her. "That's correct."

"Carla, if I may?" Dr. Green began, "We're at the point where we have to make some choices. And you can still choose how you want things to be. Normally, in cases like this, with no further options and all of our efforts not bringing on enough of an effect to stop the spread, we recommend our patients consider hospice care, prepare for the inevitable, and get their affairs in order. We suggest that they live the remainder of their days without the chemo, so they don't have to experience all those side effects."

"So I can feel better as I die."

"Mom, please. This is hard on me as well," Libby sobbed.

Carla didn't make eye contact, but she squeezed her daughter's hand tightly. "I don't like to lose, doctors."

Libby thought that was the understatement of the century.

"You've fought, and bravely. Everything we've brought to you, you've adopted and endured. You're a model patient.

Your sense of humor, just like what you're doing today, is remarkable. You haven't lost. What Dr. Nashua is saying, you can control the manner and timing of your end of days. We were hoping for more, but while we've been able to slow the spread, we've never been able to stop it. And to get aggressive now, well, that might mean more surgery and recovery and side effects, and from our tests, it shows it will not cure you. And if it won't cure you, why not enjoy the time you have left, and do it your way? Not the treatment center's way. Your way, Carla. None of us make it out alive, but you have an expiration date that is more defined. If you want to go on fighting, that's your choice. But this way, we can keep you comfortable. You'll have some good quality time to say good-bye."

Libby knew this meeting was hard on Dr. Green. Although he'd never been super optimistic about the prognosis, she felt he had truly believed that her mother would be one of the survivors.

Carla turned to her. "Libby, do you have any questions?"

Her backbone was straight. Her jaw was clenched like she was going to go on a roller coaster ride with one of the grandkids and didn't want to show how afraid she was, for fear it would scare them, too. She was meeting the news with composure. Her mother realized that the fight was over.

It was time to do the laundry and clean up the kitchen.

CHAPTER 23

COOP AND THE rest of the team were awarded a commendation for outstanding work, an initiative that was spearheaded and pushed by several victims' rights groups. The Senate convened a commission on human trafficking, which was the closest they got to some of the key players, people who actually benefitted from the trade. The U.N. Ambassador was recalled and accepted a new position as Good Will Ambassador at Large, due to his supposed expertise on the subject of the flesh trade.

And while the government's focus, along with Mexico's cooperation, was now on the sex human trafficking, the drug trade took up whatever slack had been created. Cartels operating in Eastern Europe were blamed for the huge proliferation.

Many of the chess players were moved around, but few of them were removed from the game. But one thing had remained clear, the SEALs on SEAL Team 3 were released from all liability in the mission, and a new executive order came down from the administration protecting them from prosecution in the execution of their mission.

Colin Riley himself met with Kyle and Coop one day in

Portland, where he pushed for more cooperation between their team and the private group he was building. Kyle had to decline getting more involved, but he promised to provide any assistance he could legally do. And he promised to keep his eyes and ears open and to be able to exchange some intelligence that wasn't violating their oath.

"I always knew your heart was in the right place, Riley. I just didn't see a need for a private firm to go around what the government was doing. But I see it now. It's that they are too corruptible. There's too much temptation."

"That's exactly it, Kyle. They don't have the same training, and they don't put their lives on the line like you fellas do, but they are looking to benefit from all your hard work. The day the SEALs are used on private vendettas for politicians, even presidents, is the day the SEALs will cease to be. But the argument can be made that the huge behemoth of the government is in itself a safeguard. Your small units, SEAL stealth teams who can come in and react fast to incidents, are always more effective, as long as the procuring party is not corrupt and the intel is accurate. You mess with either of those, and you've lost it. The whole country loses. So what your inquiry helped us generate was a spotlight on some of it. But it's not all of it. Be aware there are forces who may look like they benefit our country but, in actuality, are out to destroy it from within."

"Thank you, sir. I suppose you'll support any new recruits I send your way, then."

Riley laughed. "Look at it this way. You can send the recruits you want to work with in ten years on ahead, and I'll keep them busy and warm until you come join us, Kyle. There's always a place here when you're ready to do something special, not that what you do now isn't special. But there comes a time when every man decides a change of course is what he needs. Maybe not until your kids are out on their own. Maybe you see something you have to do something about, and you can't in your current situation. But some day, and I might not be here any longer when it happens, hopefully this place will still be operating as a force for good. Defender of the innocent. Benefitting the men and women and families who love freedom."

"I think it helps to know those guys are out there," Coop said to him on the flight home. "It settles me a bit. 'Cause sometimes it's a little overwhelming, isn't it?"

"It is. But that's why we train. We aren't ordinary men, Coop. And I think it came to us from birth. The Navy just organized the parts so they'd fit together to make this fighting machine. But this isn't a fight everyone can do."

THE WHOLE BROWNLEE household had discussed Carla's prognosis. Both Carla and Dr. Brownlee listened to everyone who had an opinion. Oddly, the consensus was rather wide. The family wanted the quality of Carla's last days to be optimum. Everyone agreed to help out in that endeavor.

Karen had taken a job in the San Diego area working for a sports branding and marketing firm, and since she had been such an elite athlete, the job was perfect for her. She and Coop ran the San Diego marathon, along with several other SEALs from Team 3. She also agreed to help learn about soccer and to assist Will's new team, which would start up in the fall.

The boys had a close call, nearly winning over the Catholic boys' school that came in from out of town. But in the end, they came in second. The trophy was smaller than the big one the other club got but was just as important. All of the boys had gotten a taste of what it was like to become a team, to grow with the strengths and weaknesses of all the players on their squad. Cooper made sure Will understood that's how it worked in the SEAL community as well. He saw that it was noted, a seed perhaps planted for the future.

Libby would give him hell if she knew about it.

So the decision was made to plan a big party at the Brownlee house. One last summer party of the magnitude Carla was famous for. Her imprint was all over it. It was a mixture of some of the Team guys, former Team guys, kids, Carla and Austin's friends from their social clubs, her doctors, and other patients she'd met, some of whom had received their own trophy of a possible cure or remission—things Carla was unable to claim.

But she accepted everything in good stride. Libby had pointed out, and Coop now saw, how her jaw remained clenched, her spine straight, and her eyes looking ahead. In between the great food, music, games, swimming, new friends, and the bond of humanity that connected them all, Carla made an announcement and a big request.

She passed around pieces of paper and asked everyone to put down the name of a person she should look up when she got to Heaven. She promised to convey the messages once she got there. Her final request was to love and care for one another and that she felt very full and honored to have had such fabulous friends and family.

She even warmed to Melissa, Karen's mother. She and Austin told her stories of their Will. Austin filled in the details of their boyhood together—stories Carla hadn't even heard.

Coop was proud of his mother-in-law that day and the days that passed, when the weather turned colder and rains began to show up more frequently. Nearly four months to the day she was told the treatments weren't effective any longer, she fell ill, got weaker, and passed with Coop, Libby, her husband, and Karen, as well as her nurses Annie and Benjamin by her bedside. She closed her eyes and went on to the next chapter of her life.

"Tell me, Cooper, I will be that missed," Libby said to him at the funeral.

He'd been thinking about what it would be like for them to cross that same threshold someday. "I want to go first. I don't ever want to live without you," he told her.

"Can't you imagine the conversation she's having with Will right now? He'll enjoy hearing the story about his daughter and how she was finally accepted, how she finally found her home."

Just then, he could smell the growing corn on a midsummer day in Nebraska, working with his dad, tinkering with the tractor, helping Grandpa Iversen with little Cora, and feeding the pigs. The sky was orange, but not from an oncoming murderous tornado. Because it was a glorious sunset, and they all were together again.

He smiled, and Libby asked him what he was thinking.

"I could be sad, really sad. But I think the message I'm getting is that the best way to remember them is to tell their stories, to live to the fullest we can. To take this opportunity we have to be together and make it as perfect as we can."

"To love each other," she whispered.

"Not just love…to honor and cherish each other. It is what we deserve. It is our legacy. And when we turn it over to the next platoon, they will understand that we did our jobs well."

Did you enjoy Honor The Fallen?

If you're interested in reading the first book about Cooper and Libby, please read Fallen SEAL Legacy, which is Book 2 of the original SEAL Brotherhood series.

Next in the Legacy series is Grave Injustice, coming to you later this summer. It is Armando and Gina's story, based on the book, SEAL Under Covers, with the perspective of ten years into the future.

But if you already know you want to read all of the SEAL Brotherhood books from Accidental SEAL to SEAL My Love, you can get the Ultimate SEAL Collection #1, or Ultimate SEAL Collection #2 and start from the beginning where it all began. Each book is a stand alone, but the reader will enjoy reading them in order, as they were written.

Don't forget to follow Sharon's other series:

Bad Boys of SEAL Team 3

Band of Bachelors

Bone Frog Brotherhood

Sunset SEALs

Bone Frog Bachelor

All of these books are recorded on Audible.com by the talented actor and former country star, Mr. J.D. Hart.

ABOUT THE AUTHOR

NYT and USA Today best-selling author Sharon Hamilton's award-winning Navy SEAL Brotherhood series have been a fan favorite from the day the first one was released. They've earned her the coveted Amazon author ranking of #1 in Romantic Suspense, Military Romance and Contemporary Romance categories, as well as in Gothic Romance for her Vampires of Tuscany and Guardian Angels. Her characters follow a sometimes rocky road to redemption through passion and true love.

Now that he's out of the Navy, Sharon can share with her readers that her son spent a decade as a Navy SEAL, and he's the inspiration for her books.

Her Golden Vampires of Tuscany are not like any vamps you've read about before, since they don't go to ground and can walk around in the full light of the sun.

Her Guardian Angels struggle with the human charges they are sent to save, often escaping their vanilla world of Heaven for the brief human one. You won't find any of these beings in any Sunday school class.

She lives in Sonoma County, California with her husband and her Doberman, Tucker. A lifelong organic gardener, when she's not writing, she's getting *verra verra* dirty in the mud, or wandering Farmers Markets looking for new Heirloom varieties of vegetables and flowers. She and her husband plan to cure their wanderlust (or make it worse) by traveling in their Diesel Class A Pusher, Romance Rider. Starting with this book, all her writing will be done on the road.

She loves hearing from her fans:
Sharonhamilton2001@gmail.com

Her website is:
sharonhamiltonauthor.com

Find out more about Sharon, her upcoming releases, appearances and news when you sign up for Sharon's newsletter.

Facebook:
facebook.com/SharonHamiltonAuthor

Twitter:
twitter.com/sharonlhamilton

Pinterest:
pinterest.com/AuthorSharonH

Amazon:
amazon.com/Sharon-Hamilton/e/B004FQQMAC

BookBub:
bookbub.com/authors/sharon-hamilton

Youtube:
youtube.com/channel/UCDInkxXFpXp_4Vnq08ZxMBQ

Soundcloud:
soundcloud.com/sharon-hamilton-1

Sharon Hamilton's Rockin' Romance Readers:
facebook.com/groups/sealteamromance

Sharon Hamilton's Goodreads Group:
goodreads.com/group/show/199125-sharon-hamilton-readers-group

Visit Sharon's Online Store:
sharon-hamilton-author.myshopify.com

Join Sharon's Review Teams:

eBook Reviews:
sharonhamiltonassistant@gmail.com

Audio Reviews:
sharonhamiltonassistant@gmail.com

Life *is one fool thing after another.*

Love *is two fool things after each other.*

REVIEWS

PRAISE FOR THE
GOLDEN VAMPIRES OF TUSCANY SERIES

"Well to say the least I was thoroughly surprise. I have read many Vampire books, from Ann Rice to Kym Grosso and few other Authors, so yes I do like Vampires, not the super scary ones from the old days, but the new ones are far more interesting far more human than one can remember. I found Honeymoon Bite a totally engrossing book, I was not able to put it down, page after page I found delight, love, understanding, well that is until the bad bad Vamp started being really bad. But seeing someone love another person so much that they would do anything to protect them, well that had me going, then well there was more and for a while I thought it was the end of a beautiful love story that spanned not only time but, spanned Italy and California. Won't divulge how it ended, but I did shed a few tears after screaming but Sharon Hamilton did not let me down, she took me on amazing trip that I loved, look forward to reading another Vampire book of hers."

"An excellent paranormal romance that was exciting, romantic, entertaining and very satisfying to read. It had me anticipating what would happen next many times over, so much so I could not put it down and even finished it up in a day. The vampires in this book were different from your average vampire, but I enjoy different variations and changes to the same old stuff. It made for a more unpredictable read and more adventurous to explore! Vampire lovers, any paranormal readers and even those who love the romance genre will enjoy Honeymoon Bite."

"This is the first non-Seal book of this author's I have read and I loved it. There is a cast-like hierarchy in this vampire community with humans at the very bottom and Golden vampires at the top. Lionel is a dark vampire who are servants of the Goldens. Phoebe is a Golden who has not decided if she will remain human or accept the turning to become a vampire. Either way she and Lionel can never be together since it is forbidden.

I enjoyed this story and I am looking forward to the next installment."

"A hauntingly romantic read. Old love lost and new love found. Family, heart, intrigue and vampires. Grabbed my attention and couldn't put down. Would definitely recommend."

PRAISE FOR THE SEAL BROTHERHOOD SERIES

"Fans of Navy SEAL romance, I found a new author to feed your addiction. Finely written and loaded delicious with moments, Sharon Hamilton's storytelling satisfies like a thick bar of chocolate." —Marliss Melton, bestselling author of the *Team Twelve* Navy SEALs series

"Sharon Hamilton does an EXCELLENT job of fitting all the

characters into a brotherhood of SEALS that may not be real but sure makes you feel that you have entered the circle and security of their world. The stories intertwine with each book before…and each book after and THAT is what makes Sharon Hamilton's SEAL Brotherhood Series so very interesting. You won't want to put down ANY of her books and they will keep you reading into the night when you should be sleeping. Start with this book…and you will not want to stop until you've read the whole series and then…you will be waiting for Sharon to write the next one." (5 Star Review)

"Kyle and Christy explode all over the pages in this first book, *[Accidental SEAL],* in a whole new series of SEALs. If the twist and turns don't get your heart jumping, then maybe the suspense will. This is a must read for those that are looking for love and adventure with a little sloppy love thrown in for good measure." (5 Star Review)

PRAISE FOR THE BAD BOYS OF SEAL TEAM 3 SERIES

"I love reading this series! Once you start these books, you can hardly put them down. The mix of romance and suspense keeps you turning the pages one right after another! Can't wait until the next book!" (5 Star Review)

"I love all of Sharon's Seal books, but *[SEAL's Code]* may just be her best to date. Danny and Luci's journey is filled with a wonderful insight into the Native American life. It is a love story that will fill you with warmth and contentment. You will enjoy Danny's journey to become a SEAL and his reasons for it. Good job Sharon!" (5 Star Review)

PRAISE FOR THE BAND OF BACHELORS SERIES

"*[Lucas]* was the first book in the Band of Bachelors series and it was a phenomenal start. I loved how we got to see the other SEALs we all love and we got a look at Lucas and Marcy. They had an instant attraction, and their love was very intense. This book had it all, suspense, steamy romance, humor, everything you want in a riveting, outstanding read. I can't wait to read the next book in this series." (5 Star Review)

PRAISE FOR THE TRUE BLUE SEALS SERIES

"Keep the tissues box nearby as you read *True Blue SEALs: Zak* by Sharon Hamilton. I imagine more than I wish to that the circumstances surrounding Zak and Amy are all too real for returning military personnel and their families. Ms. Hamilton has put us right in the middle of struggles and successes that these two high school sweethearts endure. I have read several of Sharon Hamilton's military romances but will say this is the most emotionally intense of the ones that I have read. This is a well-written, realistic story with authentic characters that will have you rooting for them and proud of those who serve to keep us safe. This is an author who writes amazing stories that you love and cry with the characters. Fans of Jessica Scott and Marliss Melton will want to add Sharon Hamilton to their list of realistic military romance writers." (5 Star Review)

"Dear FATHER IN HEAVEN,

If I may respectfully say so sometimes you are a strange God. Though you love all mankind,

It seems you have special predilections too.

You seem to love those men who can stand up alone who face impossible odds, Who challenge every bully and every tyrant ~

Those men who know the heat and loneliness of Calvary. Possibly you cherish men of this stamp because you recognize the mark of your only son in them.

Since this unique group of men known as the SEALs know Calvary and suffering, teach them now the mystery of the resurrection ~ that they are indestructible, that they will live forever because of their deep faith in you.

And when they do come to heaven, may I respectfully warn you, Dear Father, they also know how to celebrate. So please be ready for them when they insert under your pearly gates.

Bless them, their devoted Families and their Country on this glorious occasion.

We ask this through the merits of your Son, Christ Jesus the Lord, Amen."

By Reverend E.J. McMalhon S.J. LCDR, CHC, USN
Awards Ceremony SEAL Team One
1975 At NAB, Coronado

Made in the USA
Middletown, DE
18 October 2023